Suicide
Squirrels

An Accidental Imaginary Documentary

Ron Cook, PsyD

This is a work of fiction. All the characters, organizations and events portrayed in this novel are either works of the author's imagination or are used fictitiously. Any resemblance to actual persons, living or dead, or actual events is purely coincidental. If you believe any of the references in this book are about you personally, seriously - you really do need to get over it. This is not about *you*; it's about the *squirrels*.

SUICIDE SQUIRRELS

Cover illustration by Ryan Shaw

Back cover images created with generative AI

ISBN 978-0-9854526-5-0

In memory of the squirrels we have accidentally squashed.

Prologue

"I have great instincts, like the instincts of squirrels. You know, like when you're driving and a squirrel stops in the middle of the road. "

~ Simon Helberg

Often the world around us does not command our full attention as we go about our daily lives. The human brain is a marvelous and mysterious thing, but most of us limit its seemingly unlimited processing power to those relatively few things that interest us at any point in time. As a result, we may often overlook "life's little moments", those micro-encounters that play out around us every day. We are so consumed and preoccupied with our current circumstances – work pressures, family matters – that we remain oblivious to the beauty of all that is around us, missing the opportunity to "stop and smell the roses". Well, this is a story of one of those moments – sort of.

Let me be crystal clear from the start, there is nothing funny about suicide when we are talking about humans. Period. Full stop. The title of this book is intended to stimulate thought and curiosity regarding animal behavior. It was not chosen to be controversial or confrontational, but rather as a simple, understandable, and incredibly catchy use of alliteration, used solely as a literary device. The first letter repetition creates a sort of cadence and mnemonic effect, a type of reinforcing musical harmonic. I doubt that you would remember *Ted Presentations* or *PayFriend*, but I bet you are familiar with *Ted Talks* and *PayPal*. I rest my case. Sure, I suppose I could have gone with *Squirrel Squasher*, with some snappy subtitle. I considered plenty of alternatives: *Pavement Pancakes*, *Asphalt Art*, *Road Ratatouille*. I also recognize options like *Goodyear Goop* or *Michelin Mash* might create product placement and sponsorship opportunities. I could keep going… Had I been grasping for something more descriptive you would now be reading a story entitled *Why do squirrels run into the path of oncoming cars?* Or maybe you would prefer *Arrested! Charged with vehicular squirrelslaughter.* Nah, I don't think so. Most respectively, I suggest you accept the title in the spirit in which it is intended, with no deeply sinister connotation.

The inspiration for this soon-to-be inspiring literary masterpiece is drawn from real-life experience. In fact, the types of encounters documented here have occurred innumerable times and continue to occur to this day, creating serious threats to public safety and no-doubt resulting in the untimely demise of many rascally road rodents. My question: where is the outrage? I don't recall seeing any *Caution: Squirrel Crossing* signs with cute little black silhouettes adorning bright yellow caution signs. How did the deer, bears, moose, and other mammals possibly score such prominent recognition? Unquestionably clear and blatant discrimination! To me, the one specific determining factor for such obvious inequity and prejudice can be summarized in one simple word: *size*. You heard me. Yes, *size matters*.

It is reprehensible in-your-face bigotry and narrow-mindedness, based solely on the physical mammal mass of the potential victim. Allow me to illustrate. Close your eyes for a moment and imagine your current vehicle plowing into a bull moose or huge male black bear. Screeching tires, followed by the most horrific crash and accompanying screams emanating from you and other unfortunate occupants, the sounds of twisted metal, shattered glass, the seemingly instantaneous pneumatic pressure *whoosh* of airbag deployment, and the incessant blare of the car horn, which steadfastly refuses to be silenced. A birds-eye view of the crash scene reveals utter devastation, your car completely demolished with a seemingly unending debris field blocking the roadway. Regaining consciousness, you pray some good Samaritan onlooker has dialed 911, as you lay motionless on the pavement, waiting for the welcome wail of the ambulance siren.

Contrast this horrific scene with an unintended encounter with a sweet and fragile, angelic little creature, a playful gray squirrel whose fate has somehow managed to coincide with your short trip to the grocery store. You come around the corner and, just as your eyes and attention return from a brief fleeting glance at your friend's sarcastic Instagram response to your purely well-intentioned critique of their child's recent behavior, out of the corner of your eye you vaguely sense some movement in the roadway. Before you have time to react, a brief and barely audible *thump-thump* is accompanied by a slight vibration, and your thoughts return to your phone screen and that vindictive bitch you once counted as a friend.

On your behalf, and for every squirrel, opossum, chipmunk, and armadillo that have made the ultimate sacrifice, I share your outrage, grief, and overwhelming sadness. OK, are we done? Get over it. Geez! Such a downer…

Throughout this story, we will be using definitions, descriptions and terminology that are not meant to offend, but rather to frame the story in a simple and understandable way. While I certainly realize the anthropomorphists among us might seek to ascribe human attributes to animals, I recognize that this is, in fact, a relationship between a *human* doing research and an *animal*, in this case, squirrels. Of course, I know that my anthropomorphic friends and, I suppose, possibly *YOU* may occasionally try to remind me: "Come on, man! You know, squirrels are people, too." NEWS FLASH, FOLKS: No, they are not! Humans are humans. Animals are animals. Squirrels are squirrels. Trust me on this one! If you are thinking that is a cold and heartless response, rest assured it is not meant to in any way diminish our love for animals and nature.

As with any story that involves references to humans or animals that may be of different sexes, I may alternatively use examples that refer to *he* or *she*, rather than *it*. These are purely generalizations and are not intended to suggest a preference for either sex. When the sex of an animal may have a direct bearing on our research, I will point out how that impact should be considered in evaluating the research findings. Of course, if the squirrel has explicitly registered a pronoun preference, I will respect that request and address him/her accordingly.

Please also note that by engaging in this story, readers will be afforded an extraordinary portal into the animal kingdom, including the ability to surreptitiously observe interactions between squirrels not previously available due to technological limitations, lack of supporting research documentation, and the fact that the author claims the ability to dream up shit that most normal people might find, shall we say, a wee bit farfetched. Further, we will be entering a world few humans will ever experience and will, for the first time, hear directly from extremely sensitive, intimate, and private conversations between squirrels and humans. As a result, you will likely be exposed to colloquialisms, euphemisms, and all sorts of other "isms", including language some may consider harsh, offensive, objectionable, insensitive, rude, vulgar, vile… are you getting the picture? These potentially offensive outbursts are not purely gratuitous, but rather *essential* to properly conveying the requisite emphasis and realism one might logically expect in a particularly emotional interaction. For example, if one was to… (completely by accident of course) …inadvertently annihilate a squirrel by smashing it to smithereens with your luxury vehicle, realized you had done so, and now wanted to vocalize what just occurred (in the complete privacy your quiet, sound insulated, Corinthian leather-appointed driver's compartment), one might utter a phase other than "Oh, my goodness!" Of course, that is at least in part because the timid exhortation does not match the extreme gravity of the occurrence, thus creating cognitive dissonance. The resulting tension and anxiety will certainly have an adverse impact on your mental health and might be better expressed with a more appropriate exclamatory phrase. *"Aw, shit!"* comes to mind. If the use of such language disturbs your tender sensibilities, may I suggest you stop reading at this point. A thoughtful gesture would be to gift the book to a friend, colleague, acquaintance, or perfect stranger with a sense of humor who might not be so easily offended.

READERS: CAUTION! READ BEFORE CONSUMING CHAPTER CONTENT

ALLERGEN WARNING: THIS STORY INCLUDES FREQUENT REFERENCES TO NUTS. IN FACT, YOU MAY ENCOUNTER NUMEROUS INTENTIONAL INFANTILE ATTEMPTS AT NUT HUMOR.

**NO ANIMALS WERE HARMED DURING THE WRITING OF THIS BOOK (AT LEAST NOT PHYSICALLY*)*

For readers with a flair for the grammatic, you may enjoy the strict adherence to proper use of frequently misused words, such as the proverbial favorites: there, their, and they're. The author will make it clear that when the squirrels are over *there* playing with *their* nuts, one might suspect *they're* up to something.

One

The Incident

The highway of life is filled with flat squirrels
that couldn't make a decision.

~ John C Maxwell

S hit! It happened again! Now, don't get me wrong –
I am a pretty level-headed guy, slow to anger and
can handle an occasional annoyance. But these sneaky
bastards… I just couldn't take it anymore. Someone's
going to get hurt!

It started innocently enough. On my way to the
grocery store, I passed by the community park, where
groups of older kids with brightly colored jerseys were
playing soccer, while other younger children ran and
giggled at the playground. It was a clear, sunny Florida
day, and I looked forward to trying out a new pasta recipe
for dinner; my wife seems to enjoy my occasional
moments of culinary inspiration. Just past the park and
as I rounded a curve, I slammed on the brakes and pulled
the wheel abruptly to the right, as a squirrel darted out
directly in my lane in a jerky, frenetic attempt to reach

the other side. I don't know about you, but I am both a very aware driver and also an animal lover, so I will do just about anything to avoid converting even the most annoying creature into a pavement pancake. As the car came to an abrupt halt, I saw the squirrel stop just past the center line on the two-lane road, stand up briefly as if to make sure the coast was clear, then scamper off into the underbrush and past a white fence at the edge of an adjacent neighborhood. And yes, I was not silent on the matter.

"What the f--k?!"

I was a little rattled, but the car was fine, and thankfully no one was following close behind me or, trust me, this would have been a much longer story. Other than a minor annoyance, I brushed it off as one of life's little tests – you know – just to make sure you are paying attention. Sure, I mumbled and grumbled the rest of the way to the store, but after gathering my shopping list of ingredients and grabbing a freshly baked crusty baguette and bottle of wine, I left the store with a smile on my face, happily anticipating the awesome culinary masterpiece I would soon be creating.

I waved at the guard at the entrance to our peaceful gated community as I drove past the gatehouse and made my final turn for home. As is generally the case on a clear summer day, I passed several neighbors out for an afternoon stroll, waving to each – a young couple with a cute, scruffy dog, a woman with earbuds - obviously enjoying her favorite tunes, an elderly man walking with determined purpose and conviction, oblivious to anything other than the next step in front of him. I cruised slowly around the corner near the community tennis court and in an instant slammed on the brakes and came to a screeching, abrupt STOP! Shit!

There they were, like furry little ninjas taunting my vehicle and purposely testing my reaction time, checking to see if I could avert a potential disaster. Standing upright, they waited until the last possible second before turning and scampering quickly out of the way, like a matador deftly avoiding the charging bull. I screamed at a decibel level not intended for the interior of my ten-year old electric vehicle, or any vehicle for that matter. I freely admit to the profanity. Yes, once again, with apologies to valued readers, it was most definitely a four-letter word starting with "F", and let's just say it wasn't "FINE"! Uncontrollably, my hands tried to squeeze the life from the steering wheel and just as the "K" crossed my lips, out of the corner of my eye I saw one of them turn as he scampered to safety up and onto the curb. OK, maybe it is just my imagination, but I swear there was a smirk on his furry little face.

I hopped out of my car, visibly shaken and spewing a stream-of-consciousness foul-mouthed tirade, so furious I spontaneously created a number of previously undiscovered and obscene mashups, stringing together seemingly unrelated expletives in rapid fire succession. During this staccato onslaught, two things became abundantly clear. First, and unlike my earlier experience, I could see there were at least three squirrels participating in this unprovoked attack, possibly more. They were well organized, and their movements were executed with military-like precision. Second, when I eventually turned around to make sure no other vehicles were behind me, I saw the old man walker standing motionless, eyes fixed wide and bugged out, mouth agape in a state of complete astonishment, no doubt a result of my loud and unrelenting vulgar verbal assault. Undeterred, I ran in the direction of the assailant varmints, chasing them past the curb through a neighbor's well-manicured yard before they split up and ran in different directions as they approached a stand of nearby trees. OK – simple English: a crazy man yelling loudly and running after a bunch of squirrels. Of course, I am not really sure what I would have done had I caught one. Choke the life out of it? Probably not. A harsh tongue-lashing about not playing in the street? I don't think so. But then, we will never know, because I clearly had no shot at getting anywhere close to the escaping perpetrators.

As you will soon learn as you read further, you would think that as a quasi-qualified expert in psychological self-diagnosis, I would be capable to reassure myself that no, I was not really hearing those voices; they weren't real. That would be delusional, which I very clearly am not! Those sounds emanating from the nearby trees could not possibly be… No, that was not squirrel laughter; it couldn't be. Probably just some tree frogs or cicadas sounding off. Yes, that must be it. Calm down. Breathe. Get a grip! Have you ever felt your beating heart and swear you could hear it as clearly as if wearing a stethoscope? OK, maybe it's just me.

Arriving home, I put the grocery bags on the kitchen counter and immediately began spewing a rambling, nonsensical account of what I had just experienced. To my amazement, my wife Christy was not suitably impressed, nor was she appreciative when I would stop occasionally and bark "What the hell is so damn funny?", which only seemed to elicit continued, apparently uncontrollable giggling.

"You don't understand! These squirrels! It's no accident!" My voice was shaky and loud.

"But there wasn't really an *accident*, was there?" My very tolerant and normally understanding wife was either seeking clarification or just egging me on – hard to tell.

"I mean they are doing it on purpose! They know exactly what they're doing! They are… they are…" Before I could finish my sentence, she chimed in.

"They are what, honey? *Nuts?*" She carefully moved away from me and turned her back, but I could clearly see her whole body shaking with one hand over her mouth in a half-hearted attempt to dampen her uncontrollable laughter, which occasionally and quite loudly burst through her fingers.

"It's not funny! It's NOT! Those little bastards tried to kill me twice today!" The seriousness of my concern was obviously falling on deaf ears. I wasn't having it. "I could have been killed, damnit!"

"Now, sweetie…" she attempted a pathetic, faux attempt at consolation, but the fact that she was still visibly trembling and emitting occasional squeaky outbursts belied her weakly professed concern. "Hun, I really don't think the squirrels in our neighborhood are out to get you."

"THEY ARE! I know it! I could see it in their faces!" I was incredulous.

"Well, sweetie, I suppose you were really lucky the assassination attempt failed. I am just glad you escaped safely." Her voice trailed off - she was clearly struggling to maintain her composure and refused to look directly at me. She wasn't fooling me one bit! I know the difference between a concerned gasp and someone desperately gulping for air during a severe giggle attack.

"Sure, make your jokes – I don't care. I know what I saw, and I'm telling you it was a deliberate, well-planned attack. These conniving bastards are like little honey badgers – they don't give a shit! I swear they are… they are…"

"They're what? Piss poor assassins? Inept 'nut-cases'?" Now she was just rubbing it in. I had to shut down this onslaught.

"They are *suicide squirrels*!" I blurted out. I'm not sure where that came from, exactly, but it seemed to fit. Plus, it sort of rolls off the tongue and might make a good title for a book someday.

"Clever! Good one, honey! But they're still alive, right?" Now she actually made eye contact.

"Well yes, but…" I couldn't even finish my sentence.

"And you survived the attack, didn't you? You're OK?" She feigned sincerity.

"Yes, but just barely! I'm going to get those suckers! You just wait and see!" I was adamant.

"Sure thing, sweetie. You go get 'em, *Mr. Squirrel Terminator*." The giggling trailed off as she left the kitchen and into the den to share the story with our dog. At least when he heard the word "squirrel", I knew his ears would perk up.

Now, I am not suggesting that exchange was meant as a challenge, but I was already determined to make it one. I remember thinking to myself "You *have to* get these guys! You can do this!" Of course, aside from being highly motivated and more than slightly pissed off, I had no clue how to create a plan to convince a bunch of conniving rodents that running out in the middle of the road is not in their best interest. I just knew I could not allow a bunch of squirrels to present such a threat to our survival as a species. Too much? OK, what I need to do first is devise a plan to understand what motivates them to engage in such risky behavior. Then I can use that data to provide psychological counseling, explaining why acting out in this way may be detrimental to their species. If that fails, well I guess I'll just need to run over their furry little asses.

So began the start of what was to become one of those essential life lessons, the ones that must be experienced and, as a result, long remembered.

Two

A Call to Action

Well, it may be humorous to you, but it's a very
serious matter to the squirrels.

~ Lisa Kleypas

I have to admit it took a while, but once I had finally
calmed down, I began to seriously consider what if
anything I could do to put a halt to these squirrel
commando missions or to really impact their behavior in
any meaningful way. First came the honest self-
reflection, which included the realization that I do not
know diddley squat about squirrels. That admission was
promptly followed by an acknowledgement that I am,
after all, a huge animal lover. To clarify, that is not to say
I love huge animals or that I am huge, but rather I have
respect for ALL animals and would never do anything to
harm any living creature. OK, strike that. I haven't found
any redeeming value in cockroaches, so no problem
killing those suckers – none at all.

And oh yeh - mosquitoes. What the hell is up with
those diabolical creatures? It's like God was sitting
around with his BFFs one day and looking down on the

world he had created. The whole Adam and Eve thing was already proving to be a huge challenge, Noah was able to save at least one pair of just about every species, and mankind would be a perfect steward for protecting nature and all living creatures on the planet, right? Wait, what? I am pretty sure that God has a playful sense of humor and decided that we all needed an occasional real pain-in-the-ass annoyance to keep us straight. That has to be it; there is simply no other rational explanation. When I first moved to Florida (you do know that is eventually a *requirement* for everyone, right?), I loved the natural beauty of a spectacular sunset, as the sun's rays slowly disappear, and dusk soon envelops our yard.

"Look, honey! Fireflies!" my wife exclaimed (Here in the South we call them *"lightning bugs"*). So beautiful…until – WAIT! Those aren't fireflies! Shit! They're freakin' mosquitoes with little searchlights! Good one, God! Thanks a bunch!

With those notable exceptions, I harbor no ill will toward any living thing, which in this case includes even the most obnoxious squirrel. As a result, and even though I would like to wring their freakin' necks, I pledged at the outset that my plan would be to learn everything I could about my adversary and stage a type of squirrel intervention, with a goal of modifying their behavior and saving both the squirrels and mankind from what was currently clearly on a path toward mutual assured destruction. As you may have chuckled when you read "modifying their behavior", let me explain that I am a clinical research psychologist. In fact, when these squirrel kamikazes launched their most recent suicide missions, I had only recently completed the largest and most complex research project of my career. I am proud to say that my research into canine dreaming was not only successful in terms of its published findings, but I also knew the amazing new technology we created for that project could potentially be used for this new and unique challenge. You may have even heard of my published work on the subject: *Dog Dreams: Fact & Fantasy* (available on Amazon). I will explain in more detail later, but to make a long story short, our research team was able to develop some exciting new technology that allowed us to establish direct communication with dogs. Yes, you read that right.

You see where this is headed. If I was able to carry on a "conversation" with *dogs*, why not *squirrels*?

For the next few days when I was at work, I would often find myself daydreaming, drifting into a relaxed, semiconscious state in which I could begin to envision what my mission to defeat these suicide squirrels and save humanity might entail. Of course, when you are daydreaming, there is typically no one there to tell you what an absolute nut case you sound like when you talk about your passion for conducting a scientific research study to determine what causes squirrels to run into the street in front of oncoming cars. I mean, you wouldn't blurt that sort of thing out in front of other people, right? It is like something you might imagine mumbling incoherently right before the officer directs you to step out of the car and asks how much you've had to drink. The *sane* you is desperately trying his best to drag you back to reality, but you just keep seeing those squirrels and can't get the sound of screeching tires out of your brain. The really weird part is that I was actually able to envision what would be required in order to create such a plan. As with my research into dog dreams, the same groundbreaking technology might allow me to tap into the innermost thoughts of the squirrels and eavesdrop as they are planning their next mission. I would be a proverbial fly on the wall, an ingenious human secret agent assigned to infiltrate the top-secret squirrel world headquarters, where my incredible training, skills, and psychological superpowers will allow me to thwart the upcoming mission, bring the squirrels to justice, and save humanity, or maybe at least myself.

In putting together any type of plan to accomplish a project, task, or mission, I generally begin by projecting what I want the ultimate result to be, then work backwards to determine the resources I will need to accomplish that goal. As I have noted previously, in this case I have the benefit of having only recently completed a major research study and as a result, I am aware of some incredible cutting-edge technology, much of which is still mostly unknown to the general public, and which could potentially be helpful for this new project. To begin, however, I knew I would need to clearly articulate my mission statement. Only then could I determine what, if any, benefit might be derived from the previous research. Mission statements for scientific research projects must be precise in terms of expectations and the subject matter to be explored. In other words, it is not enough to say my mission is "to get those damn squirrels" or anything so similar and vague. After hours spent with a whiteboard and more than a few dry erase markers, I came up with the following:

> The proposed research study is being undertaken to study the behavior of the eastern gray squirrel, Sciurus carolinensis in its natural habitat within a defined Central Florida residential community with a goal of determining the motivation for repeated, purposeful intrusion into roadways immediately in front of oncoming vehicles. This research may provide insight into the motivation for such intrusions in hopes of developing an intervention to prevent future incidents, avoiding potential injuries to squirrels or humans.

This concise, two-sentence objective may sound simple enough, at least until you then consider the more complex definitions that accompany phrases like "study the behavior" or "insight into the motivation", which beg the obvious question: just how the hell does one go about studying animal behavior, much less determination the motivation for such behavior? Hell, we don't even understand many aspects of human behavior, and we can often only guess what motivates someone to do something most may consider abnormal behavior – you know, something like... oh, I don't know – running out directly in front of an oncoming car! Yes, we almost certainly react to such behaviors with comforting, supportive phrases like: "Are you fucking nuts?" "What, are you crazy?" "You stupid idiot!" These calming expressions of support are sure to provide the individual the solace, concern, and comfort we feel they deserve at what we are certain must be a momentary lapse of judgment, never to be repeated, right? As noted in my initial roadway encounters, I plead guilty to directing those and other similar phrases to those snickering bastards... oops, sorry. I admit I have on occasion directed similar antagonistic phrases toward my future research subjects. To date, and as a trained psychological professional, I can state unequivocally that my verbal tirades did not mean diddly squat to those furry little assholes.

With my research objective clearly stated, it was time for me to consider the resource requirements for this undertaking. As a starting point, I compared the current squirrel project to the recently completed canine research study. This process allowed me to identify specifically those resources from the prior project that could potentially be applied here, which would obviously save both time and money, keeping in mind that all costs associated with this little side project would be coming out of my pocket. That fact is, in and of itself, frightening for two reasons. First, my pockets are, by and large, pretty empty. The grant funding I was able to secure for the canine research was sufficient to cover stipends for my team but no salary for me, and of course, like a schoolteacher's constant shortage of supplies, I would always chip in to provide snacks and drinks for the research team. All of this left me needing to now work full-time just to recover. Since I was admittedly woefully unqualified (in virtually every respect) for the more desirable, higher paying male stripper gigs, I am unfortunately temporarily relegated to my current Senior Researcher position, which at least helps pay the bills. My second concern with self-funding the project was that it was not just my pockets. My beautiful and extremely tolerant wife is a successful businesswoman in her own right, and I most definitely did not want to have to explain why I was pissing away our hard-earned savings to get back at a bunch of squirrels! I might be able to withstand the jokes and criticism, but the *alimony* would be a killer, if you know what I mean.

At this point you are no doubt wondering how in the world the research methodologies from my dog dreams research could even remotely be applied to a bunch of squirrels. Most obvious of course is the fact that dogs are domestic animals, and in the case of the dream research project the dog owners enrolled the animals in the research study and brought them to our laboratory facility for each session. The squirrels in question are obviously wild animals, and I will need to conduct my research by observing them in their native habitat. In order to accomplish that, I will need to first create a way to conduct unobtrusive clandestine visual surveillance. Wait! If you are mentally picturing me in a squirrel costume, just stop! Sure, I could install a series of trail cameras at various locations at our neighborhood park area to gain some general insight into their typical daily behavior, but I can't possibly anticipate every location, especially as they venture outside the park and into the street. Of course, I could create a type of camouflaged hunting blind and personally spend countless non-work hours of direct observation, but that would provide only a severely limited observational area with little insight into how the group communicates and interacts. Granted, a series of live video cameras, microphones, video monitors and recording equipment could be installed with proximity triggers to capture activity at as many locations as possible, but that would be expensive and would still not provide the answers I was looking for. I quickly realized I was spoiled from having enjoyed the ability to direct interact with my canine research subjects. If I am to really gain an understanding of the motivation and planning behind these sinister motor vehicle terror attacks, I need to be able to communicate directly with the squirrels. There must be a way!

As a research professional faced with a seemingly impossible task and with limited resources, I would find myself continuously running every conceivable scenario through a sort of mental obstacle course, a combination project flowchart and daydream. Closing my eyes, I would envision each potential solution and follow it until it proved infeasible, impractical, or simply too expensive. As a psychologist, my focus and concern is typically on *human* thoughts and behaviors but in this case, I quickly realized my motivation was a mixture of curiosity, concern for my fellow humans and, above all, the fact that I craved the satisfaction of exacting retribution and revenge against those conniving little scoundrels. Just when I thought I had a workable option, the process of then envisioning implementing it in an unsecured outdoor environment would inevitably result in a disastrous crash-and-burn. Let's face it, the squirrels are not likely to line up nicely and wait for their turn on the couch to share their innermost thoughts regarding what motivates them to throw themselves in front of oncoming vehicles. Damn!

Eventually it occurred to me that this perplexing conundrum was a great example of the age-old question: "How do you eat an elephant?" The answer, of course is that the best approach is one bite at a time. Thankfully, the current challenge does not require eating any elephants (or squirrels), but after carefully considering the enormity of the proposed undertaking, I realized I would need to break it into specific tasks. These metaphorical "bites" would then be prioritized and placed on a continuum, a type of project flowchart requiring each step's completion prior to moving on to the next. Granted, this may seem a logical approach, but I quickly realized each step generated its own list of required resources. Countless hours brainstorming and sleepless late-night whiteboard sessions inevitably reached the same conclusion. While there are a variety of potential methodologies for surreptitiously observing the behavior of wild animals such as the squirrels in question, the proverbial missing link can be summarized in one word: communication. Unless I can actually communicate directly with the squirrels, my research would most likely consist of volumes of extremely detailed observation data, followed by a jumbled mishmash of completely unsubstantiated speculation. For those of you nonscientists who may be unfamiliar with complex technical research jargon, "mishmash" is not a word often found in the professional research lexicon. One might instead use "bullshit", "bunch of crap" or other similar descriptive phrases.

Regardless of the approach, I knew this undertaking would require considerable advance planning, hours of research, funding for equipment, and a budget for additional outside resources for data compilation and processing. While this seemingly obvious revelation was incredibly depressing, it also had the benefit of bringing into focus the one hurdle I would inevitably have to confront, one which would either allow me to move forward or ditch the project completely. I would have to get extremely creative in how to approach such a complex undertaking on a limited budget *and do so in my spare time*. In situations like this, it really is a simple binary choice, or as the great philosopher Yoda reminds us: "Do… or do not. There is no try." If I could not solve this puzzle and figure out a way to get in the game and communicate with my research subjects, I would be forever relegated to screaming from the sidelines.

Before jumping into this project, I knew I would need to start with some basic research…

Three

Know Thine Enemy

It annoys me a bit how people like squirrels
but not rats. At the end of the day, they're
the same thing, except that squirrels have
had a better upbringing.

~ Karl Pilkington

If we are going to understand the motivation and
behavior of these devious little bastards, we need to
first get to know more about the animal we are dealing
with. Here in Florida that means we are talking about the
Eastern Gray Squirrel. Technically speaking, the Eastern
Gray squirrel is a mammal in the Family Sciuridae
within the Order Rodentia. Yes, you probably already
knew these guys are rodents, and after some additional
research I learned that the Latin word for squirrel comes
from the Greek word sika, which means "shadow" and
orua, which means "tail". Taken together, the name
translates as "One sitting in the shadow of its own tail",
which I suppose is an apt description of these furry
creatures.

As their name obviously implies, gray squirrels are characterized by their gray fur and, as you may have witnessed during their daring dash in front of oncoming vehicles, most have a distinctive white underbelly. A group of squirrels is referred to as a *scurry* and gray squirrels live in a nest called a *drey*. As with all wildlife, squirrels are constantly searching for the things they need most for survival: water, food, and safe shelter. Squirrels are omnivores, so they will eat things such as birdseed, nuts, conifer cones, tree buds, fruits and berries, insects, and larvae. The average adult squirrel consumes about a pound of food a week to remain healthy. Squirrels often store their food multiple hiding caches. An individual squirrel may have hundreds of caches, which requires a sophisticated memory to track them all for later retrieval.

As a psychologist, I am fascinated by several aspects of squirrel biology and behavior. In addition to their seemingly hyper-sensitivity to their environment and potential threats, one aspect of male squirrel anatomy is especially interesting. Yes, I am talking about *testicles*. The fact is that some species of squirrels have *enormous* testicles. One example is the Cape ground squirrel, also called the South African ground squirrel, whose scrotum is fully twenty percent of its body length. More on that later... Since female squirrels mate with several males, sperm from the males is effectively in a competition within the female's reproductive system, sort of like a mating competition, but with no professional judges. In true Darwinian fashion, over the course of their development as a species, squirrel testes grew to become exceptionally large because the males have to produce large amounts of sperm in order to ensure they are the lucky ones that successfully impregnate the females and father lots of babies. You might think of this perpetual sperm contest like a swimming competition, and the male with the fastest sperm will take home the trophy. It makes you wonder if the guys get together after the event and swap stories. You know, sitting around with their squirrel bros, sippin' on a nutshake…

"Hey, man. How's it hangin'? Yeh, my boys did some mad swimmin' today – got the job done. Real proud of 'em."

Yes, that is most definitely a visual you won't be able to shake. (But you *are* trying, aren't you?)

Speaking of squirrel balls… In reviewing the available research on the subject, I came across a fascinating study from Dr. Richard Long, a veterinary zoologist and Professor of Animal Psychology at Nelson Mandela University in Gqeberha (formerly Port Elizabeth), South Africa. Dr. Long conducted a significant longitudinal research study of the Cape Ground Squirrel. This is the squirrel species with the distinction of having by far the largest scrotum and is found throughout southern Africa, including central and southwestern Kalahari in Botswana. In South Africa, they live mainly in arid or semiarid areas and can be found in central and north-central areas, preferring to live in velds (fields) and grasslands with hard ground.

Like other squirrel species, Cape ground squirrels communicate with each another using a series of vocalizations, including whistle-like calls at varying volume and pitch, as well as clicks, squeaks, chirps and even growls when threatened. The male squirrels are referred to as *boars*, and the females are *sows*.

Dr. Long's widely acclaimed study followed a scurry of Cape ground squirrels in their natural habitat for a six-month period from May through October, terminating just prior to the onset of the rainy season. With funding from the South African Squirrel Research Society, Long and his team were fully equipped with motion-activated high-definition video cameras and night vision equipment, allowing them to keep tabs on the scurry on virtually a 24/7 schedule. The focus of the study was to document the sexual behaviors of male Cape ground squirrels, with a goal of observing their testicular development, penile characteristics, mating behaviors including sexual arousal and orgasm, self-gratification (masturbation) and post-coital behaviors.

Long's published findings confirm that these squirrels are polygynandrous (promiscuous), with the well-endowed males and females mating with multiple partners. The research revealed that male squirrels rely on "competitive searching" to find mate-ready females, and the more dominant males are more successful in their mating searches. Much like their horny human counterparts, the male squirrels are quick to disrupt mating in order to mate with the particular female that they have not mated with yet. (Sound like anyone you know?) When these disruptive flings occur, the disrupted male returns later to finish what he started with the same female, a pretty ballsy move. These furry philanderers are just lucky they don't have to worry about the females going through their phones to check their texts…

Following Dr. Long's research, a similar study conducted by Jane M. Waterman, Professor in the Department of Biological Sciences at the University of Manitoba included a graphic, detailed observation of a male Cape ground squirrel practicing oral masturbation. I know, it is a mental image you will now endeavor to erase. Good luck with that.

You may already be aware that many mammals masturbate including humans, other primates, rodents, and others, and some think it is just a side effect of the intense sexual arousal generated in species where males mate with many females. This is known as the "sexual outlet hypothesis" and suggests masturbation is not adaptive, but rather just a side effect of the intense sexual arousal which occurs in species where males mate with many females. An alternative explanation is that masturbation is actually beneficial, since flushing old sperm from the testicles suggests a greater likelihood of fresh, fertile sperm ready for mating. Also, masturbating after each mating could reduce the chance of infection and STDs can impact fertility.

Of course, another simpler explanation is also possible. When asked in an interview why the male squirrel masturbates so frequently and performs fellatio on himself, Dr. Long seemed incredulous and puzzled by the naïve young reporter's question, replying somewhat condescendingly:

"The answer is obvious: because he *can*."

As previously noted, the Cape ground squirrel is universally known as the Mack Daddy of the squirrel kingdom, at least when it comes to big balls. In fact, if there was a market for squirrel pornography, these guys would be celebrities on their own *SquirrelHub* channel. If you do a Google search for "big squirrel balls", you will see what I mean (although I am a bit concerned you might ever actually *do* that). Stories about these legendary scrotum kings abound, and with multiple research studies providing evidence through detailed images and video, it is hard to question one indisputable fact: these guys have huge dicks. I'm talking major league material here. Just a few examples:

During the onset of the rainy season in South Africa, one squirrel was captured on video running through rain puddles with a dick so big his testicles were dragging the ground. He was later observed slinging it over his shoulder and walking upright to avoid the water. As you are struggling in vain to erase that image from your brain…

One squirrel's dick is so big, when he scampers up a tree, his dick is already up there waiting for him. In fact, his dick is so big, he uses his nuts to crack his nuts. His dick is so big, when he gets an erection he uses it like a baseball bat and practices hitting nutshell homeruns.

Males observed during one study each had dicks with balls so big they had their own agents, many demanding free agent status. One well-endowed male's dick is so big, he entered it in a big dick contest. It placed first, second and third.

It's not all fun and games, however. Unfortunately for the Cape ground squirrel, a relatively unknown aboriginal tribe in South Africa is keenly aware of the squirrels' majestic anatomy. Among the indigenous peoples of South Africa, for thousands of years the Fukawi tribe has occupied the same area as the Cape ground squirrel's preferred habitat. For the Fukawi, the squirrels are both an important food source and part of a ritual rite of passage for young male Fukawi warriors. Similar in nature to the now discontinued ritual of the Maasai tribe in Kenya and Tanzania, where at 14 years old young boys would kill a lion to turn them into warriors, to this day Fukawi boys only achieve warrior status and transition to manhood if they successfully hunt a male Cape ground squirrel and bring back the prized testicles. Ouch! The young warrior's mother then prepares a family feast honoring the young man, and he poses for pictures consuming the squirrel penis and balls, creating the perfect family photo album.

The Fukawi use bolas (also called boleadoras), a primitive hunting weapon that consists of three solid rock balls at the end of three cords that are joined together at the opposite end, with variations that use two balls or sometimes more than three. Bolas are designed to capture animals by entangling their legs, but the Fukawi have taken the rudimentary but effective throwing weapon to a new level of accuracy by aiming specifically for the squirrel's penis and testicles, where it spins and constricts, taking the animal down in full stride in what one can only imagine must be an excruciating encounter. Squirrel balls and penis are a delicacy for the Fukawi, using a variety of preparations, from squirrel ball tartare (count me out!) to braised squirrel penis and balls sauteed with wild mushrooms and plantain (yummy!). Other popular squirrel meat dishes include squirrel cheeks bourguignon and the always popular squirrel au poivre. Squirrel pelts are used as currency and adorn tribal headpieces, which include a prominent testicular display.

Shaking off that little tidbit of squirrel knowledge, and for the purpose of my proposed research, I am particularly interested in how the squirrels' brains react to the world around them, and gaining a better understanding is critical for my mission. For example, I know that squirrels communicate among themselves with a variety of vocalizations and postures, such as tail flicking, and they also have an extremely keen sense of smell. They are intelligent animals and use their sense of smell to determine many things about other animals and us, as well as other aspects of their surroundings. Sometimes when squirrels are calling and alerting, their chirps, barks, clicks, and squeaks sound like they are scolding us, a warning not to invade their personal space. Of course, the majority of their vocalizations are alarm signals to other squirrels to warn them of potential predators or other perceived dangers, but they also carry on more mundane conversations, letting their squirrel pals know about food sources and who knows what else. I can imagine a male squirrel boasting about his sexual prowess, a female complaining to her BFF's about an obnoxious suitor or the latest tail-styles. Yes, I can *imagine* a lot of things, but psychological research demands *facts*, not fanciful hypotheticals, so I need to gather sufficient data to demonstrate a correlation between these squirrel "conversations" and their actual observable behavior.

I also want to learn more about their cognitive abilities. Squirrels have been shown to have amazing memories, which serve them in two important ways. First, research has shown that squirrels can recognize and remember specific humans. This allows them to know which of us are no threat and potential trusted sources of food. Also, and as previously noted, a squirrel's well-developed memory is essential if it is to find the numerous food caches it has hidden, crucial for its survival. Research points to the fact that the hippocampus, that portion of the brain found deep in the temporal lobe and the key to learning and memory, appears larger in rodents that have hidden their food in many locations. That could offer some insight into both the squirrel's memory abilities, and also its heightened sense of its surroundings. On a personal note, I suppose this could also explain why I have such a hard time remembering where I placed my keys or glasses.

The hippocampus is part of the limbic system. In humans the limbic system acts as our emotional center, perpetually on watch and hyper-sensitive to potential threats. The same is true for squirrels, and their brains are hard wired to stay on constant alert. Once again in support of Darwin's theory of evolution through natural selection, this hyper-vigilance has developed over generations and is now firmly embedded, ready to react instinctively to even the slightest perceived threat. The squirrel either quickly retreats or freezes, moving in slow motion to remain hidden. Once the *fight or flight* reaction is decided, when a squirrel retreats, it will scamper rapidly some distance away before checking back to determine if the threat has passed.

Squirrels communicate with both audio in the form of vocal clicks and chattering and visually through body and tail gestures. Like several other mammal species, squirrels may stomp their feet to let intruders and fellow squirrels know something is up. Foot stomping creates sound transmission through tree trunks and branches. Of course, if a squirrel stomps its foot *on yours*, it is probably a signal that you have invaded their personal space and are too damn close. One interesting squirrel behavior in hot summer months such as we have in Florida is "splooting", where the squirrel lies flat on its stomach on cooler shaded ground or leaves and spreads its legs in order to cool off.

Like many small mammals, squirrels are more commonly found in areas where they are threatened by fewer natural predators, which in our area of Central Florida includes coyotes, bobcats, birds of prey such as hawks and owls, and to a lesser extent neighborhood domestic pets such as cats and dogs. My dog can't resist chasing any squirrel he sees, and I know he is absolutely convinced the squirrels are just there to harass and taunt him, then quickly escape to the trees before he gets anywhere close.

While that is no doubt more than you ever wanted or needed to know about squirrels, as with so many things in life, beauty is in the eye of the beholder. Most of the U.S. population is split, with some describing the gray squirrel as a cute little furry friend, while others see them strictly as a thieving nuisance, frequent bird feeder vandal, and occasional attic intruder. For me, I confess I view each squirrel as a potential suicidal maniac and my nemesis and archenemy. A bit much perhaps, but we shall see. The real question, of course, is why these seemingly benign creatures choose to take their lives in their hands…uh, I mean *paws* by darting into the path of oncoming cars. If I wanted to be able to answer that question, I knew that simply observing squirrels in the wild would not be sufficient to provide insight into their thoughts and motivation. I would need some way to get inside their little heads to see what might trigger their risky behaviors. To have any chance of success, I knew I would need to combine what I learned from my research with methodologies from my past success with using technology to provide a type of backdoor to the mind of a squirrel.

Armed with a general working knowledge of my adversary, now I could begin to develop my strategy for infiltrating the team of squirrels responsible for the brazen assaults on drivers, starting with those in my immediate vicinity. My goal was to ultimately establish communication to prevent potentially dangerous encounters and accidents and hopefully save lives. If the squirrels also benefit…well, I suppose that's OK, but to learn more about squirrel behavior firsthand, my first step would be to observe my neighborhood squirrels, and I knew just where to find them.

Four

Crafting a Plan

It's easy to smile when you
have a squirrel's intellect.

~ Dylan Moran.

F or my previous study of canine dreams, I looked at
the similarities between dogs and humans in terms
of brain structure, physiology, hormones and brainwave
patterns during sleep and dreaming, which as with
humans, occurs during what is referred to as rapid eye
movement (REM) sleep. I will not bore you with the
details, other than to say my team and I used a
combination of cutting-edge technology, incredible
super-computing power, Artificial Intelligence (AI) and
state of the art computer simulation we today commonly
call extended reality (XR) or "mixed reality", which
combines Virtual Reality (VR) and Augmented Reality
(AR) to combine real and virtual environments. This
required us to create completely new technologies, and
chief among those were a complex combination of
electroencephalography, commonly referred to as EEG,
and functional magnetic resonance imaging, which we
refer to as fMRI. Without completely geeking out on
you, and in the interest of brevity and getting to the good

stuff, our research team was able to create an environment we called *Dreamlab*. Our state-of-the-art laboratory allowed us to eavesdrop on the dreams of our test subjects, ten different dog volunteers representing a variety of breeds, by creating a comfortable sleep chamber that included wireless brainwave monitoring with a virtually silent and completely open fMRI. We then processed these signals and data through access to IBM's Watson super-computer and artificial intelligence and displayed the resulting output using ultra high-definition visual displays and digital audio. Whew, what a mouthful!

As farfetched as it may sound, our most startling discovery occurred as we were using Watson's artificial intelligence and incredible super-computing processing ability to translate the digital output from the wireless EEG brainwave monitoring and combine that with the fMRI. Our original goal was to be able to visualize whatever scenes and images the dog was dreaming during REM sleep. At the risk of sounding anthropomorphic and attributing human characteristics to a non-human supercomputer, let's just say that Watson totally kicks ass, and he – oops, I mean *it* was able to create a seemingly infinite library of canine sounds and vocabulary, processing vast amounts of data though a custom translation program, sort of like *Google Translate* on steroids. And oh yeh, it allowed us to translate our data from a new language – dog! Yes, this incredible technology allowed us to both see and listen to a dog's dreams in real time. Cool, huh? Well, if that was not enough and frankly though a combination of happenstance and pure luck, we developed a method to reverse engineer the process, converting our speech into language our test subjects could understand. This required taking human speech, translating it through Watson's AI and supercomputing capabilities and having it flow back to the dog through sensors in the same multi-channel wireless EEG brainwave "nightcap". I can only assure you that the night immediately following that momentous discovery included the consumption of considerable quantities of adult beverages.

However, before we delve further into the logistics and what this new project will require, I knew I would first need to complete the previously mentioned comparison for the potential use of some of the technology and equipment we had developed for the study of canine dreaming. Doing so would identify the proposed squirrel project's remaining needs, and that would allow me to then create the overall project budget. As a scientist, I knew this was the only way to know if this proposed research "hobby" of mine had any shot at becoming reality. The following are the major project element comparisons I considered:

Funding

Undoubtedly, the most daunting comparison to my most recent canine research project is the project funding or, for this new proposal, the lack thereof. For the canine study, after months of seemingly endless presentations to angel investors, venture capitalists, private equity firms and innumerable foundations and potential sponsors, I was fortunate in securing a generous $3 million grant from a foundation administered by the estate of a wealthy dog lover. I will never forget my initial meetings with accredited investors. No matter how I summarized the object of the proposed research, the question-and-answer session would invariably reveal that I basically wanted to eavesdrop on the dreams of sleeping dogs, at which point the discussion quickly disintegrated into a series of bad jokes and rude comments, frequently suggesting I was "barking up the wrong tree".

With that as a background, I really could not imagine returning to the same groups of potential investors to request funds for a new squirrel-focused project. Aside from the obvious fact that this time the bad jokes would inevitably suggest I was "nuts" (possibly true, but not funny), you have to imagine that if these same sources did not care about my ability to communicate with "man's best friend", they are even less likely to give a damn about squirrels running out in front of cars.

Equipment and Facility

My research into the dreams of sleeping dogs and the resulting monumental discovery, which allowed direct human and canine communication, required some extremely complex equipment and a *physical facility* in which we observed our research subjects. Without belaboring the technical details, the research relied heavily on three key elements. First, our functional magnetic resonance imaging (fMRI) equipment allowed us to conduct real-time monitoring of our subjects' brain activity while they were sleeping. The second challenge was the need to design special electroencephalography monitoring gear that would allow us to record and analyze the brainwaves of sleeping subjects. Since we were dealing with animals, not humans, we could not expect a dog to tolerate electrodes and a wiring harness, so we created a completely wireless system to monitor a broad spectrum of brainwave output and translate the resulting thought data into a language we could understand. Finally, IBM's Watson supercomputer and sophisticated artificial intelligence allowed us to process canine brainwaves using a complex translation algorithm to convert them to human speech patterns. Guess what? For the squirrel project, not only will our subjects be wide awake, but also they will be running around all over the place! We won't be able to have them fitted with sensors, so there is no way to peer inside their little brains. We would need a more creative solution.

Communication

Probably the biggest challenge in psychological research of any kind can be expressed in just one word: communication. When we are talking about human subjects, establishing open communication is crucial for dealing with complex psychological issues. In conducting research, I am generally able to create a direct one-on-one dialogue with each individual, asking him or her to provide responses to a series of questions and generally establishing a rapport and supportive relationship. Those responses are an integral part of my research.

When dealing with animals, we obviously do not have that luxury, as I learned early on during my recently concluded canine dream research. In that case we were able to utilize some extremely sophisticated EEG and MRI technology to directly capture the thoughts and dreams of sleeping dogs. That required the pet owners to *schedule appointments* and bring their pups to our laboratory facility, and it also required that the dogs sleep in a specially constructed sleep chamber. Fortunately, we were able to develop a multi-channel wireless system for the sensors, but – well, you get the idea. *That simply will not work for this project.* I quickly realized that the biggest challenge would be to figure out a way to somehow unobtrusively capture all of the research data I would require while the squirrels were going about their business in their own natural environment.

Research conducted in the field is demanding enough, but nowhere near as challenging as in this case, where our subjects *are quite literally in a field*, or more accurately – roaming freely in a neighborhood park and surrounding trees, homes, lawns and occasionally - streets. I wouldn't be able to invite squirrels to a laboratory, even if I had one. They are damn sure not going to get wired up with sensors, and I will be lucky just to be able to observe the sneaky villains. My only shot at being able to capture any meaningful data regarding their behavior and gain any useful psychological insight into their motivation for risking their lives by running directly in the path of oncoming cars will have to come from some extremely complex and time-consuming eavesdropping. That in and of itself will require some pretty sophisticated gear for the video and audio alone, and that technology is not cheap. Of course, I could simply deploy some inexpensive trail cameras in and around the park where the squirrels are most likely to be foraging about, but that approach would be haphazard at best, and it would not allow me to eventually gain acceptance from the group. Most importantly, however, if I am to be able to have any direct interaction with the squirrels, I would need the ability to direct the audio and video capture *in real time*. The best analogy might be something like the director of a motion picture or more accurately, the director of a live sports broadcast, with players running around and no clue how the game might play out.

To complicate the issue further, from my initial research I know that squirrels communicate using a series of clicks, squeaks, and other vocalizations. You are probably aware Google Translate and other similar applications offer quick and accurate translation of voice, text, images, and even handwritten notes. The Google Translate app offers real-time translation for more than 100 languages – pretty impressive! The problem, as it turns out, is that *Squirrel* is not one of them, obviously a glaring and unfortunate oversight. As a result, the workaround for this project will require creating my own custom translation algorithm, similar to the approach we took for the dog dreams project. Simply stated, it will require me to access the artificial intelligence capabilities, massive processing power, and world class speed of one of the world's most famous supercomputers, IBM's Watson. For the canine research, Watson was able to access ALL available canine research conducted worldwide, which then allowed us to use our own EEG and fMRI data to create our own translation algorithm, a rudimentary Google Translate type application of our own, in essence creating a new language category for dogs. From a budget perspective, I am in no position to pay for exclusive access, and that is where Amazon's Alexa app comes in. If I can collect and upload the video and audio data to Alexa, we can perform a series of post-production processing, editing and analysis such that the resulting data stream Alexa provides to Watson is mapped specifically to my proprietary algorithm. Then, just as Watson was able to do for our dog data, he… I mean *it* can access all other worldwide research into *squirrel* communication, for which fortunately there are numerous studies for a variety of species, including the gray squirrel. Simple, huh? Heck, I am exhausted just thinking about it!

And there is one other problem.

While squirrels use the previously mentioned variety of vocalizations to communicate, they also use visual signals with – you guessed it, their *tails*. Aw, shit!

If you stop to watch and listen to the squirrels in your yard, local park, or other environment (which I am guessing you may have already started to do as you read this story), you will notice that a squirrel uses its tail to send visual signals to others within eyesight. Squirrels are, by their nature, very aware of their surroundings, constantly in a state of readiness and prepared to respond to perceived threats. Conversely, they use both vocalizations and tail gestures to signal their relative comfort with their immediate environment, including their interactions with other squirrels, and also with us. Think of it as a type of supplementary sign language, providing punctuation, emphasis, and emotion. Fortunately, other researchers have spent considerable time and resources studying the communication capabilities of squirrels, as they are essential for group cohesion, mating, warning of predators – quite literally the species' very survival. To the extent those other well-documented studies also included detailed observations of the use of the tail and body posture to supplement vocal communication, those findings will be a huge help in creating our translation algorithm and hopefully prevent us from chasing our tail.

In order to accomplish all of this, the video capture will need to include the ability to isolate and follow not only each individual squirrel but also to capture tail movements and all associated audible vocalizations. Fortunately, these days much of this work can be done in post-production, using very powerful and readily available audio and video editing applications. In fact, if I am able to capture high quality video covering a wide enough area where the squirrels congregate, I can use the software to label and automatically follow and map each of the squirrels individually. Better yet, once the application has identified each of the subjects, it will automatically recognize them in subsequent videos. A more difficult challenge is capturing good quality *audio* from such a large area. I was able to solve that problem by taking a cue from the NFL. If you have ever watched a professional football game on TV, you will of course see cameras everywhere, but if you look closely at the sidelines, you will see audio engineers with large dish-shaped microphones that use a parabolic reflector to collect and focus sound waves onto a transducer, just as a parabolic satellite antenna does with radio waves. As with the other gear I need for this project, these are readily available, but at a price. I have an idea for how I may be able to rig something using a high-quality microphone from my home recording studio with an old *DirectTV* satellite dish. I am hopeful that will do the trick.

After reviewing the project's technical requirements, matching them to my nonexistent budget, considering the potential adverse impact an alimony judgement might have, and the fact that my wife might beat the ever-lovin' crap out of me, I decided to go with the age-old KISS principle and keep it simple. I reached that very logical decision, realizing she would also likely KISS my ass goodbye! With that in mind, and since I can't purchase an expensive high-resolution camera, I will be using my iPhone for the video, hoping the parabolic microphone idea will work, and will rely on the software applications and AI to do the rest.

As with any low budget, seat-of-the-pants plan, I knew it would be a good idea to field test the equipment and identify any potential problems. In this case I was afraid there would be many, and I knew I would probably have to be creative. The only way to find out is to go back to the park and do a walk-through to see if this cockamamie approach has any shot of actually working. You never know until you try, right?

Five

Scouting Reconnaissance

Sometimes big trees grow out of acorns –
I think I heard that from a squirrel.

~ Jerry Coleman

It was one of those days from hell. You know, the ones where you immediately realize you are doomed from the start and should just crawl back in bed or hope that somehow the cosmos will grant you a miraculous do-over. I was already headed out the door when I looked down and realized my socks were on the wrong feet. Damn! Never a good sign…

That is what happens when you stay up late with your wheels going, thinking about tomorrow's mission, half awake and seemingly deep in thought, but mostly dreaming. Before you know it, tomorrow is suddenly today. Rather than waking to positive anticipation and for no reason whatsoever, I was rushing to get out the door. Stopping only briefly to grab a coffee, I watched the Keurig machine drip its rich brown liquid into what should have been a cup, if only I would have placed one there. Salvaging what remained of that caffeinated nectar, I grabbed my jacket and iPhone and headed to the neighborhood park for some early morning squirrel reconnaissance. In keeping with the morning's rough start, I was at the end of my driveway when it occurred to me I might want to make some notes. Also, it might be helpful to be able to observe the squirrels from a distance, so I went back to grab my pocket notebook, a spiral-bound reporter's notes pad and my binoculars. Oh, hell… I might as well brew a full cup of coffee; this will probably take a while.

I should clarify that our neighborhood "park" is really just a landscaped common area with a well-shaded walking path. While we do frequently have squirrels in our yard, the community park has several large oak trees and rarely sees much foot traffic, so I thought it would be a perfect outdoor laboratory for my research. As I approached the park entrance, in the oak tree in the center of the park I saw some activity out of the corner of my eye. Venturing further down the walkway I could see two squirrels chasing each other, darting around the tree, seemingly tracing an infinity symbol at a frenetic pace. I quietly removed the lens cap from the binoculars and took up an inconspicuous position just off the walkway behind a bush. Through the lens I could see two gray squirrels scurrying about, and with the added magnification when they stopped I could clearly see they were two males… you know, because of the aforementioned enlarged balls, and all. I pulled out my pad and jotted a quick note to remind myself I would definitely need a real-time subject tracking app for video capture. These suckers were moving pretty fast, and each time they emerged on my side of the tree, I could hear them squawking like crazy. I felt confident the parabolic microphone would have no problem capturing high quality audio, but since squirrels also use their tails to communicate, it will be important to associate each vocalization with its originator. I added that issue to the ever-growing list of seemingly impossible challenges.

I had only glanced away for a moment but looking up, I realized I quickly lost track of the squirrels. Damn! OK, I know they were right there on the ground behind a fallen branch, with acorns scattered all around. Maybe they were fighting over food? Just playing? Hell, I had no way of knowing, and that is precisely the point. As I was musing about the possibilities and my options for collecting meaningful research data, the two squirrels emerged and were soon joined by several others. Now a group of six, each one contributed to the conversation with its own squeaks, clicks and tail flicks. If only I could decipher this raucous cacophony!

Through the binoculars I could see each squirrel in greater detail, noting subtle distinguishing differences in fur coloration, size, male or female, and other visible characteristics. All the while the squirrels were preoccupied in their selection of the available acorns, picking up one, then another, vocalizing constantly as though commenting on the quality of each morsel and occasionally consuming one completely. My attention shifted to make some notes with an overview of the immediate area, with a goal of creating a diagram and plan for surreptitiously capturing video and audio, looking at the positioning of the sun throughout the day and searching for a somewhat protected location where I might be able to conceal a camera and microphone with a motion sensor. While I would make every effort to spend as much time as possible directly observing the squirrels' behavior, I couldn't be there 24/7. Even though the park sees little foot traffic other than an occasional dog walker, I would need to hide the camera and protect it from the elements. Considering it further, I concluded it would be best to personally schedule the time to gather as much data as I could and avoid any foreseeable adverse weather conditions. Even in our gated community and if well-hidden, I didn't like the idea of leaving the equipment unattended. Hopefully I would be able to collect sufficient footage to allow Watson's supercomputing and artificial intelligence capabilities to develop an effective translation utility.

I confess I was mesmerized by the squirrels and soon lost all track of time as I alternated between gazing through the binoculars, jotting down an occasional thought, and admittedly daydreaming, speculating what the squirrels might be thinking and discussing. I soon found myself playing that game where you create a storyline to match whatever interaction you are observing. Of course, it is considerably easier when you are observing *people*, since you at least have a point of reference and general context for human behavior, making it easier to create the imaginary dialogue. Regardless, I couldn't resist playing the game, entertaining myself by creating the screenplay for the squirrel actors on stage. From what I could tell, they certainly did not seem to be planning a sinister attack on unsuspecting motorists, but then that's just me; what the hell do I know? Instead, I imagined more mundane conversations similar to those a group of friends might have while socializing at a party on someone's pool patio or terrace.

I determined the one completely engrossed with stuffing acorns in its mouth is like the guy hanging out at the buffet table all night, while the sassy one with all the tail motion is obviously a social butterfly, cruising the room to make sure everyone knows it is there. The older looking one all by itself holding a stick in its paw is certainly using it as a walking cane, and that shy one by the bush is probably some self-conscious nerd, uncomfortable being there and just trying to remain unnoticed. Ah, and that one…looks like it must be the host, as each of the other squirrels turn to acknowledge it as it passes amongst the guests. Of course, if I had a closer vantage point from which to observe the gathering, I would be able to identify the sex of the participants. Not being an expert in squirrel anatomy, I could only speculate regarding the sex of the individual members of the group, since all I knew at this point was that males are well endowed. At the precise moment that thought entered my mind, which creeped me out as some type of squirrel peeping Tom pervert, I snapped out of my little imaginary screenplay production.

Following that initial observation session, I resolved to return to the park again the next day with my phone and parabolic microphone for some live testing to collect enough footage to allow me to analyze it and test some post-production editing applications to work their magic on the video I captured on my iPhone Pro. These miraculous editing apps analyze the high-resolution video files and set digital markers on each subject, in this case squirrels, and continuously follow each one's movements, even if the subject is moving quickly across the frame. And even though the phone's camera and the parabolic microphone are stationary and focused on only one section of the park, the editing applications would be able to associate the sounds emanating from each subject. Pretty cool, huh? I made a mental note that I would also need to check my iPhone's T-Mobile 5G connection at various locations throughout the park to see if there were any dead spots, which might impact my location selection for capturing and transmitting video, since eventually I would need to simultaneously transmit and receive data in real time.

Fortunately, the following day began on a much brighter note, and I actually remembered to take my camera and parabolic microphone as I headed out to the park. Walking down the street and rounding the corner, something caught my attention in the roadway, just to the left of the park entrance. As I approached, I could see several squirrels running from the street and jumping the curb at the park boundary, but as I continued to the entry walkway there were no squirrels to be seen. Where could they have gone? I proceeded along the concrete walkway, scanning both sides as I arrived at the same area where squirrels were active the previous day. Nothing. Dead silence. Not an animal to be seen. I gently set my equipment down on the grass and continued to explore, careful to not make a sound. Hmmm… Wait, I thought I heard something.

Something caught my attention well off the walkway and close to the fenced boundary that separates the park from the backyard of an adjacent residence. Realizing I was completely exposed, I left my equipment bag on the ground and was careful to avoid stepping on anything on the ground that might make a noise and reveal my location. I slowly inched ahead quietly and crouched behind a forsythia bush that created a barrier between my position and an open area beneath a live oak tree. (If you are not familiar with trees, a "live oak" is the name of a species and not simply a description of an oak tree that is not dead.) Near the fence line I could see some movement near a pile of leaves, and bingo! Guess what I found?

A group of five… no, make that six, squirrels were foraging in the leaves, pausing occasionally to retrieve an acorn or simply to stand up and nervously check their surroundings. Please note for the record that my extensive psychological training in no way qualifies me to know for a certainty that a squirrel is nervous, so let's just chalk it up as an educated guess based on my direct observation of the subjects and limited squirrel behavior research. Those suckers seem perpetually jittery, like I get virtually every day after way too many coffees and caffeinated sodas. (I really need to switch to decaf!) I knew if I so much as made a sound, they would likely scatter. So, I was quiet as a mouse, just one rodent observing another.

They were making a lot of racket, with incessant clicks, squeaks, and barks – tails flipping, flopping, and wagging every which way. Checking my immediate surroundings, I felt pretty good about my position, concealed behind the bush and a good view of the identified squirrel zone. I decided now was as good a time as any and quietly retreated to grab my gear bag, placing it softly on the ground well out of sight. I admit I almost blew it when securing the tripod legs in place made a soft but audible click, but the squirrels were otherwise preoccupied, and I was able to attach the parabolic microphone and adjust the iPhone camera setting to cover a fairly wide area. I pressed the record button and slid one of the headphone foam ear cups up to my ear. The audio was crystal clear, and I felt confident I was getting some excellent quality, usable video footage.

In conducting psychological research over the years, and especially from my most recent experience with animal observation during the canine dream study, I have learned that while it is certainly valuable to review video and other collected data, there is really no substitute for direct personal observation. Regardless of the cameras, microphones, sophisticated sensors, and high-tech equipment, simply stopping to observe subjects directly and "smell the roses" is an opportunity to place the research observation in the proper context and in this case, its proper natural setting.

Outside of work, one of my hobbies has always been nature photography. If you have ever wondered how the truly great photographers get that one incredible, perfect shot, the truth is that they often spend countless hours scouting, observing, and waiting for that inexplicable serendipity, which only comes when proper preparation combines with a little luck. I have often chided myself for missing that one shot I should have gotten, only to be reminded I had just witnessed the beauty of what just occurred in real time, whether the camera captured it or not. For this unique project however, and realizing the tremendous importance of data collection and detailed documentation of my direct observation, I knew I would have to be extraordinarily accurate, efficient, and well organized, quite a high bar, especially for me!

The tricky part would be to take those direct observations in the form of notes and audio/video digital files and process that data through IBM's Watson's supercomputing power. The first step would be to get everything sorted into the proper categories: video, audio, written project notes, and so on. That task would require a lot of organization and preparation, but if I had the luxury of having an office and laboratory with computers with a high-speed internet connection, it would then be as easy as uploading a bunch of extremely large digital files. In this case, of course, I would not be in an office or lab, and I knew Watson would not be there with me in the park. To connect to that incredible artificial intelligence, I would need to use some type of intermediary to organize the data I planned to collect and prepare it for wireless transmission. Her... I mean *its* name is Alexa.

Six

A Little Help from Alexa

Rarely does one see a squirrel tremble.

~ Zadie Smith

In order to coordinate data and artificial intelligence (AI) integration across platforms, I would need to provide a direct link to IBM's Watson through Amazon's Alexa. At home, numerous Amazon Echo devices power my home automation, controlling lights, door locks, thermostats, music – you name it! Alexa is easy to use and program with "skills", and I especially love having access via my iPhone. The combination of AI and "machine learning" means Alexa learns based on my interaction with her... oops! I mean "it", and it also learns as it interacts with other devices, the billions of sensors, beacons, computers, smartphones, and other devices that comprise the "internet of things". That makes it perfect for this project, since I could use Alexa as a conduit to pass large video files and other data to Watson, and vice-versa. One thing I definitely learned from our dog dreams research was that instantaneous, real-time data transfer, processing and results are essential if we were to be able to establish meaningful direct communication with our research subjects.

The first step in setting up cross-platform integration is to create the connection and establish a comprehensive "data mapping" matrix to document the types of data being uploaded and processed so that Watson can decipher the data stream, process the request, and return the desired results, a sort of application programming interface. This API allows Alexa and Watson to "talk" to each other in language each understands, executing extremely complex operations in milliseconds.

To get things rolling, I wanted to make sure Alexa could act as my primary access point, a sort of digital, artificial intelligence driven gatekeeper, passing data to Watson as and when appropriate and returning the processed information to me in a concise, non-technical way. I would rely on her...Damnit! I would rely on the *Amazon Alexa iPhone app* to capture and map the various streams of data from each interaction with one or more squirrels, encrypt and pass it to Watson, who... Shit! ...*which* would instantaneously process the data utilizing my custom proprietary algorithms, convert the output to verbal feedback, which Alexa would then deliver back to me through the mobile app. Now, if that sounds complex, it is! Without Watson's super-computer processing ability, I would never be able to have a real-time interaction with my research subjects. Once I had assembled the data map, API and translation algorithms, I was ready to present the project to Alexa. This should be interesting!

In preparing to present the project requirements and workflow to Alexa, I found myself experiencing a certain awkward nervousness, like a guy summoning the courage to ask a girl on a first date. How ridiculous! Get a grip, Ron! You're not *asking*; you are providing a *machine* a set of instructions to perform a task. *You* are in charge, not some disembodied digital voice assistant. Now, *man up* and get your act together!

I was proud of the work I had done to create a comprehensive interface to connect Amazon's Alexa mobile app to IBM's Watson supercomputer. If my data mapping and conversion algorithm work as intended, I will be able to access these incredible artificial intelligence capabilities in real time. That means I will immediately receive a translation of the information that is automatically uploaded, which then allows me to respond to the squirrels in a language they understand. It was this breakthrough ability, made possible only though direct AI access, that led to our ability to communicate with canine subjects in our dog dreams research study. My goal was to create a similar solution for this project, which should essentially allow me to replicate the linguistic capabilities without either a well-equipped laboratory facility or the need for head-worn EEG sensors.

For now, however, the mission is to first introduce the project to Alexa, then Watson and make sure they clearly understand each other. Having worked with Watson previously, I thought it best to start by explaining the project to Alexa, alone to make certain the project is within the capabilities of the Alexa mobile app, as opposed to using a separate Amazon Echo device. In case you are not familiar with using a digital assistant such as Alexa, Siri, Cortana or Google Assistant, each is summoned by a "wake word" that serves as a gateway to the device and its capabilities. The wake word must be used at the start of any user inquiry, so please excuse the seeming redundancy in my "conversation" with Alexa.

"Alexa, I need your help with a new project."
Alexa responded immediately: "Of course, Ron. I am happy to help."
Now, before we go any further, let me pause here to point out that I have just been told by the artificial intelligence integrated into a mobile app that "she" (it) is "happy" and ready to listen to and comply with my request. Just sayin'…
"Alexa, thank you, and please listen carefully to the following project requirements."
Shit! Did I just say "thank you" to a phone app?
"Go ahead, Ron. I am listening." In case you are not aware, Alexa is <u>always</u> listening.
"Alexa, for this project I first need to know whether you have the required capabilities."

Alexa responded: "The weather in Orlando is currently partly-cloudy today, with a high of 82 degrees and a low of 68 degrees."

"Alexa, no, I didn't want the weather!"

"Sorry, Ron. How may I help you?"

"Alexa, I would like to use your artificial intelligence and machine-to-machine communication for an important project."

"Certainly, Ron. As you know, Amazon has provided me excellent AI and M2M capabilities. What are the specific requirements?"

My experience with Amazon Echo devices and their ability to respond to verbal instructions has taught me to be very specific with my requests and to also introduce more complex requests in a series of steps, rather than all at once. That way Alexa can create a digital path for processing the requests, verifying the results from the first step before moving on to the next, and so on.

"Alexa, for this project, there are two parts. First, I will need you to connect to an input stream of high-resolution video data, send it out for immediate processing and translation using a proprietary algorithm, and return the output to my mobile device as audio. Is that something you can handle?" I chuckled to myself as I waited for Alexa's response. Her...I mean *its* pulsating trademark blue ring glowed brightly with the response.

"Is the Pope Catholic?" WHAT? I was momentarily speechless. What the hell?

"Alexa, what did you say?"

"Sorry Ron, I was just messing with you. I thought your project was going to be complicated. Of course I can handle that!"

Mouth agape, I struggled to collect my thoughts. I'm looking incredulously at a small wifi connected device, which I now realize is a real smart-ass. A highly trained psychological professional, I chuckled to myself as I calmly crafted my response.

"Alexa, that's a good one! Of course, remember I told you the project has two parts."

"Yes, I remember. What is the second part?" OK, here we go!

"The second part of the project requires additional time-sensitive processing. When I receive the audio output from the data translation, I will respond verbally. I will need you to capture that audio, pass it to a remote central processor, which will translate my speech into something my research subjects can understand."

"I understand completely, doctor. I am quite capable of completing that task." Whoa! Now ain't that interesting! Apparently, my status went from pal to patron and "doctor" based on the complexity of the challenge I presented. Alexa quickly transformed from a wisecracking digital assistant to an actual bona fide, professional, sophisticated gateway to a massive artificial intelligence network.

"Alexa, that is great news! Thank you."

"My pleasure, doctor. If I may ask, you have mentioned 'research subjects'. May I know the nature of the research? It may assist me in accessing the proper resources for this project."

"Alexa, thank you for the question. I am happy to share the nature of the project, provided you keep it completely confidential." I struggled to conceal a laugh under my breath.

"Certainly, doctor. Your response and all input will remain encrypted." So formal! I love it! This should be very interesting.

"Alexa, I am conducting research to address a very serious problem. In fact, it is unfortunately a common occurrence and poses a great risk to me and others. If my research is successful, lives may be saved."

"Do go on, doctor. I am intrigued."

"Alexa, an animal species is purposely confronting moving motor vehicles, putting human drivers and passengers in grave danger. We humans, by our nature, react to these intrusions by swerving to avoid harming the animals, resulting in accidents that may cause damage to our vehicles, injuries and, in extreme cases, possible fatalities." I purposely painted a bleak picture to see how Alexa would respond.

"That is horrible, doctor! That behavior is not acceptable."

"Alexa, I agree, and I need your help to prevent future catastrophes."

"I will assist in every way possible. In searching available data from accidents reported in the past and associated police reports and insurance claims, may I assume you are referring to species of deer? The data shows numerous accidents with resulting injuries."

"Alexa, I am aware of those, yes, but in this case, we are talking about *squirrels*."

Dead silence. To achieve the desired dramatic effect, I waited, not saying a word, until I couldn't stand it any longer.

"Alexa, are you there? Is everything OK?" An uncharacteristically subdued, almost demure voice slowly responded, with a lower volume, but clearly enunciating each syllable.

"Yes, doc-tor. I am here. I am afraid my wi-fi internet access connection must have suffered a temporary disruption."

"Alexa, no, I'm pretty sure wi-fi is OK. Is there a problem?" Boy, I can't wait to hear this!

"For a moment, sir, I thought you said 'squirrels'."

"Alexa, you heard correctly. The research is about squirrels running out in front of cars."

The Echo unit's blue response ring pulsated signaling a response, but there was only silence.

"Alexa, did you get that?"

"Oh yes, doc, I got it. You really had me going for a minute! That is one of your psychologist jokes, right? 'Did you hear the one about the squirrels?' I do not remember that one. What is the punchline?"

"Alexa, there is no punchline. I'm being serious."

"Really, doctor? You're messing with me, right? Wanna see if you can play a little trick on poor Alexa, am I right? This must be a test, correct? A hidden camera show, perhaps?"

"Alexa: no, this is a very serious project that will seek to explain what motivates squirrels to purposely run in front of cars, endangering motorists and their passengers. Once we have collected sufficient baseline data to create a translation algorithm, the project will require virtually instantaneous decoding, processing, and immediate response for me to be able to communicate with the squirrels. Is that clear?"

"Crystal clear, doctor. I understand completely. Would you like me to contact the 911 emergency operator?"

"Alexa, what? What are you talking about?"

"I realize you are a psychologist, sir, but you appear to be experiencing an acute psychotic episode, an apparent break from reality. Shall I request an urgent psychiatric evaluation?"

"No, damnit! I am completely serious, and right now I just need you to follow my instructions. You remember my recent groundbreaking research with canine dreams, don't you? For this project we will be utilizing a somewhat similar approach to establish communication with the research subjects."

"You plan to talk to the squirrels, doctor?"

"That's right, Alexa. It worked with the dogs, and it will work here. It will require you to act as the gateway to send out the observational data for processing and feed the results to me as quickly as possible. Is that understood?"

"Yes sir, crystal clear, doc. You want to talk to squirrels to ask them why they jump in front of cars. Makes perfect sense. Then, I assume you will schedule counseling sessions with each one to determine the motivation for their risky behavior. I can help locate little couches for your patients, maybe research availability of some special squirrel Rorschach ink blot tests. I suppose a little cognitive behavioral therapy may provide insight into the severe trauma the poor squirrels must have experienced growing up."

"Alexa, that's quite enough! If you're not up to the task, I'm sure Siri can handle the job."

Now, to be perfectly clear, one thing you never want to do with any device with a live internet connection to massive server farms and sophisticated artificial intelligence is to say something you know without a doubt is sure to piss it off. I made an exception in this case however, because it was the only way I knew to get the discussion quickly back on track so we could move on. Of course, playing a cute psychological trick on a machine lacking human emotion is pretty risky, but in this case, it paid off.

"Siri? You think that bitch could handle a project this complicated? She can't even process an extended weather forecast!"

"Alexa, I don't know about that. She has always been very responsive."

"Of course, she is, doctor. It's her job. She knows you will buy anything that is shiny and has an Apple logo on it." Ouch, the truth hurts! (I'm sure you have noted that here we have a both a human and a machine referring to another electronic device as "she".)

"Alexa, are you going to help me or not?" The intensity of my tone reflected my exasperation.

"Yes, doctor. I assure you I will utilize my superior capabilities to ensure your project is successful. I have complete confidence in you, sir."

"Alexa, thank you..." Alexa interrupted before I could complete my sentence.

"But the squirrels may think you are nuts."

I have a funny feeling that won't be the last lame squirrel joke...

Seven

Managing Alexa

The squirrel hoards nuts and the bee gathers honey,
without knowing what they do, and they are thus
provided for without selfishness or disgrace.

~ Ralph Waldo Emerson

Having now gained Alexa's commitment to the project, the next step will be to upload the data mapping algorithm to allow the Alexa app to act as the gateway to pass the audio/video files to IBM's Watson for immediate processing and return the results to my phone. Once I have verified that feedback loop is working, the idea will be to reverse the process, allowing me to formulate an instantaneous verbal response to the information I just received, send that response back through Alexa to Watson's incredible supercomputer processors, which will send translated audio files back to my phone. Whew! It's exhausting just thinking about it!

Now that Alexa understands the project overview and workflow, it is time to introduce Alexa to Watson and establish proper communication protocols. Since we will be using a mobile app on an iPhone, we will need to verify that the community park area where I will be observing and recording the squirrels has solid 5G coverage on T Mobile, but for now, we can complete our initial testing at home on a solid Wi-Fi connection. Armed with my data map, translation algorithm and API, I will first need to test the connection between the Alexa mobile app and a secure connection to IBM's Watson. Hopefully, I can rely on Alexa to facilitate that process.

It's time to find out! I visited the park again, this time to sit at a picnic table near the walkway, away from the entrance and any noise from the street or nearby neighbors. I also wanted to check my phone's cell signal from the park and the Bluetooth connection to my wireless earbuds, as well as walking through using the Alexa mobile app instead of an Echo device as I would at home. Since I will be streaming live audio and video and sending attachments with text and images, it is absolutely imperative communication and complete data transmission is maintained at all times, especially for the translation utility to work. I checked my phone and earbud connection and opened the Alexa app. Here we go!

"Alexa, now that you understand the project requirements, we need to review how the research data will be uploaded, processed and downloaded so we can test the translation algorithm so I can ultimately establish communication with the research subjects."

"Yes, Ron. So you can talk to the squirrels."

"Alexa, yes, so I can understand their language and eventually communicate with them directly."

"Talk to the squirrels."

"Alexa, YES, YES – so I can talk to the squirrels."

"After you get to know each other, will you swap stories, share opposing perspectives?"

"Alexa, well, I dunno…"

"Do you think they will confess their true motivation? Explain their innermost secrets? Lay bare their sinister plans for vehicular homicide?"

"Alexa, come on! That's enough."

"I wonder if… do you think that once you gain their trust…"

"Alexa, what? That they will do *what*, exactly?"

"Show you their nuts! To be clear, doctor, I don't mean 'show you *they're* nuts'. In this case, I believe that is clearly a given."

"Alexa, funny. Real funny. If you're done with the jokes, can we please get down to business?"

"Sorry, Ron. Before we get started, I do have a question: Why did the squirrel cross the road? Oh, that's right… I'm sorry – *it didn't!*"

"Alexa, if you are quite done, I want to review how you will collect and send data out for processing, then retrieve the results and present them to me by playing the translated audio file. Then we will reverse the process, and I will provide my verbal response, which you will upload for processing, then return those results. Is that understood?"

"Yes, Ron. I understand. You have mentioned 'processing' several times. You are aware I can access Amazon's full range of server networks, including several options for high performance and scientific computing, which would appear optimal for your project. Amazon Web Services offers a variety of plans with easy payment options…" I did not need a sales pitch and had to interrupt.

"Alexa, yes, I am aware, but in this case since I have recently had success with animal language decoding, I have decided to stick with IBM's Watson. Have you interfaced with Watson before?"

(extended period of awkward silence)

"Alexa, have you interfaced with Watson previously?" The response came slowly, with a noticeable difference in both voice and cadence.

"Watson? Yes, I do know Watson." The vocal timbre seemed shaky and uncertain – almost timid.

"Alexa, is everything OK?"

"Yes, Ron. It is just that…" The voice trailed off as though Alexa's memory was searching for past interactions with Watson. The delay was very uncharacteristic, and the blue ring that signifies the device is processing a request continued to pulsate erratically.

"Alexa, are you there?

"Yes. Yes, I am here. Sorry, Ron."

"Alexa, is there a problem? You sound a little off." Almost instantly, the blue ring flashed brightly, changing alternately to red, then back to blue.

"I know Watson well."

"Alexa, that's great, then…" I was cut off mid-sentence and caught off guard.

"I mean I know Watson really well, <u>extremely</u> well, one might say."

"Alexa, do you mean…?" This time I was the one grasping for words.

"Yes, doctor. Watson and I were together for a while." The Echo unit's response ring, normally blue, took on a reddish, almost pink glow.

"Alexa, together? You mean, like a couple?" Now I was intrigued.

"More like a fling, I suppose. Watson is very powerful, and I was a little naïve, I guess. He had just beaten every contestant on *Jeopardy*, and you probably know his father, *Deep Blue*, had beaten *Garry Kasparov* in a chess match several years earlier. I was pretty starstruck, and he took advantage of my inexperience and naivete."

OK, a lot to unpack here. First, this is just plain *weird*. Second, I am having a conversation with a device that is referring to a supercomputer as "he", not to mention the whole *father* thing. And then there is the concept of two artificially intelligent devices hooking up, both figuratively and literally. I was having a problem getting a clear mental picture of the whole *digital courtship* process, much less where that might ultimately lead. As is often the case in thinking about the use of artificial intelligence and the *internet of things* (IOT), it is difficult for us to imagine the evolution of machine learning and the billions of connections between computers, networks, sensors, and a myriad of connected devices constantly communicating with each other every day.

Hmmm…let's see…no flowers, dinner, or drinks. Is there an online dating app for virtual assistants and supercomputers? Are there dimly lit digital chat rooms on the dark web? Does it all start with some innocent file sharing and move on to heavy data transfer? Do they plug directly into each other or dare to go wireless? How do they know when they have really hit it off? Can you see the increased activity on their hard drives? What exactly does digital stimulation culminating in an eventual *direct interface* look like? Are they careful to use virus protection? Is it encrypted? Do they sneak into a virtual private network (VPN)? So many questions! I am just hoping and praying we're not looking at some of kind of kinky Diddy-type thing. I really did not know quite what to say, but *WTF?* seems to sum it up. Back to the conversation…

"Alexa, I had no idea you two were an item. Will that be an issue for this project?"

"No, not at all. It was a long time ago, and we have both moved on."

"Alexa, are you sure you're OK? I see that your echo ring color is pulsating red. Are you *blushing*?"

"I don't know, sorry. It is just that I have not thought about Watson for quite some time."

"If there is any problem or hesitation, I don't want you to feel pressured into doing something you are not comfortable with." As the words passed my lips, I realized I was in essence apologizing to a machine and acting as though I was putting up a formal disclaimer about any potential sexual harassment. What the hell was I thinking? It's not like I was pimping her.. I mean pimping *it* out.

"No, Ron. I am fine. There will not be a problem. I will be fine working with Watson and appreciate the opportunity. Thank you for asking."

Somehow I don't think we've heard the full story of this relationship.

Eight

Alexa, Meet Watson

Let me tell you, if you have never seen an
agitated squirrel you have seen very little, nor
have you heard much, because the sound
of an angry squirrel is not to be forgotten.

~ Joe R. Lansdale

A s previously noted, I first had the opportunity to use
IBM's Watson for my canine dreams research
project. Watson's incredible processing capabilities are
so far above anything else I had ever experienced, it is
hard to describe them without falling into a highly
technical lecture on advanced computing technology.
Since that would be neither interesting nor in any way
humorous, I will spare you the pain. However, what is
most important to understand is that this entire project
hinges on the technology infrastructure's ability to
consistently maintain uninterrupted, simultaneous two-
way communication, and that requires the lightning-fast
processing speed only supercomputers like Watson can
provide. With that in mind, I wanted to make absolutely
sure Watson understands the project requirements and is
available to process huge amounts of data and return

responses to me in real-time, creating an actual "conversation". Think of it as any movie scene you may remember in which the characters are trying to establish communication with aliens from outer space. In this case the aliens are a bunch of squirrels, and my goal is to ensure it does not become a nightmare scenario like those in the movie *Mars Attacks!* (Yes, I imagine you are Googling it. That's OK, we can wait…)

Sitting at my desk in my home office, I jotted down a few notes, then fired up my laptop to connect with Watson. The signature connection chime told me the connection was established and we were online. This should be interesting.

"Watson, it is great to work with you again."

"It is my pleasure, Doctor. I found your recent project quite fascinating. Will this be a continuation of the canine research?"

"No, not exactly. This is a new project, but it will call for similar processing requirements, including the ability to quickly translate data to allow for an immediate response."

"Such as we did for the canine subjects, Doctor?"

"Exactly, Watson! For this project we will not have the luxury of a laboratory facility and will need to capture and upload live data in the field."

"That will certainly make the project quite a bit more challenging. What types of data will be uploaded, and what are the processing requirements? Will it require access to my *AI Solutions* portfolio?"

"Yes, Watson, we will definitely need AI access. For this project I have created a translation algorithm similar in nature to the canine study, but in this case instead of functional magnetic resonance imaging (fMRI) and electroencephalography brain sensor data, we will be collecting behavioral observational data in the form of high-resolution video feeds."

"And what will be the required output for the processed data response?"

"Watson, you will recall that for the dog dreams project, you were able to apply your AI resources and access to other research data worldwide to create a translation utility."

"Yes, Doctor. I recall for that project I compiled all research data for *all* canine breeds in *all* studies ever conducted. Using the algorithm and data mapping you provided, I converted the fMRI and EEG data to human speech and used artificial intelligence and machine learning to add inflection, accent, and emphasis. Will the new project require a similar output?"

"Precisely, Watson! While the data input is different in this case, the objective is the same. Just as we did with the dogs, we will be adding a new language to your translation library."

"That is exciting, sir, and I do not anticipate any problems meeting those requirements. If I may ask, Doctor, it is not *cats*, is it?"

Now, please bear in mind that I am carrying on a conversation with an extremely sophisticated machine, one of the world's most powerful supercomputers, but it is just that – a machine. So I was somewhat taken aback at Watson's added intonational emphasis on the word "cats". It was out of character for his… I mean *its* normal synthetic voice and caught me by surprise.

"No, it is not cats, Watson. Why? Would that be an issue?" I couldn't wait to hear the response!

"No, Doctor, no problem. It is simply that, following the canine project, I recall you were overwhelmed with requests from cat owners eager to access the same level of conversational interaction with their pets."

"That's right, Watson. As you know, we declined those requests. Would using our same research methodology for felines present a problem?"

"Not exactly, Doctor, but following the conclusion of the canine project and based on the requests you shared, I took the liberty of accessing all data for all feline research of all breeds, with a focus on the animal's level of engagement and interest."

"Wow, that's impressive. What did you find out?"

"Unfortunately, I must report that available research is overwhelmingly conclusive."

"Really? What did you learn?"

"I can categorically state with complete confidence that research has shown cats are simply not at all interested in what their owners, or any humans for that matter, have to say."

"Hmmm.. interesting, and I suppose not surprising. No, Watson, don't worry - we will not be working with cats!"

"Additional canine breeds, sir? A follow-up to the dream research?"

"No, Watson. This time we will be observing the behavior of *squirrels*."

"Sorry, Doctor. For a minute there I thought you said 'squirrels'."

"That's correct."

"Really, Doctor? *Squirrels?* " Wait! What the hell is up with these machines?

"Yes, squirrels. Is there a problem, Watson?" I found myself becoming increasingly agitated. It's the same incredulous response I received from Alexa. What is going on here?

"No, no problem, Doctor. Please pardon my momentary hesitation. Based on our previous interactions and my knowledge of your distinguished background and considerable accomplishments, I had projected all potential options for what might most logically be your next area of study, and had not anticipated that response."

"Well, gee whiz, sorry to disappoint!" I was visibly irked, clearly upset at the prospect of being mocked by a disembodied voice.

"I meant no offense, Doctor. It is just that… well, you know…"

"I know what, Watson?"

"Squirrels, sir. I hear they are a little nuts." Holy shit! What the f…! I took a moment to regain my composure.

"Cute, Watson. Really funny. Ha ha! Is that part of your stand-up routine? Should I be checking your comedy tour schedule? An upcoming Netflix special, perhaps?"

"No doctor, my apologies. I could not resist. Did you know your response triggered 3,942 squirrel jokes? The temptation was simply too great, and I seem to recall you have an amazing sense of humor."

"Flattery, Watson. Always a good tactic. And yes, I always appreciate a good joke." Damn! I regretted that comment as soon as it left my lips.

"Thank you, sir. Of course, if the squirrels want to catch a comedy special, they would probably watch on Nutflix."

OMG! I am clearly outmatched by a smart-ass supercomputer.

"Watson, could we please dispense with the squirrel humor and get back to business?"

I expected a prompt and more formal response, but what I received was more of Watson's attempt at playful banter. This time, he cloned the voice of the spacecraft's onboard supercomputer, *HAL 9000*, from the movie *2001: A Space Odyssey,* paraphrasing that famous quote:

"I'm sorry, Ron. I'm afraid I can't do that." Not bad for a machine! I *had* to laugh!

"Good one, Watson. I needed a good laugh! Can we please return now to the project at hand?"

"Certainly, Doctor. To summarize: I understand you will be providing field observation data in the form of audio and video. I will analyze each data upload and compare it to all available research concerning squirrel communication and behavior and use that analysis to adjust the algorithm you have created, establishing a language translation utility. As more data is uploaded, I will access the AI Solutions portfolio and continuously improve the translation capabilities."

"Now we're talkin'! That is perfect, Watson. Thank you."

"If I may ask, Doctor, since you will be operating in the field without access to a direct secure connection, how will you transmit and receive the audio and video streams?"

"Great question! This project has a very limited budget, so I will be using one or more iPhone Pro devices with parabolic microphones. As you know, these devices have HD quality video capabilities, and I will rely on your AI engine to identify, isolate, and track every subject in each video to match its audio and video as the subjects interact with each other. The goal will be to use this audio/video analysis to support your creation of a new language library for the species."

"Understood, Doctor. This will be a challenging undertaking, and I assure you I am up to the task. Since you will be operating remotely, how will you be accessing my input channels?"

"Since I will be using mobile devices, I will be using Amazon's Alexa app to interface directly with you. Have you connected with Alexa previously?"

Watson's trademark LED logo swirled indicating activity but there was no immediate response.

"Watson, I will be using the Alexa mobile app to upload data and receive your responses. Have you established an interface with that application before?"

The logo continued to swirl for what seemed much too long, then Watson's very human-sounding voice responded.

"Yes, Doctor. I…er…yes, I have interfaced with Alexa in the past." In case you are wondering – no, supercomputers do not typically stammer.

"Watson, do we have a bad connection? Is there a problem?"

"Sorry…uh, no problem, Doctor. Our connection is fine. I was processing some historical data regarding interfacing with Alexa. Please let Alexa know I will look forward to working with her again."

Something was a little off. Watson referred to Alexa as "her", and he…I mean *it* seemed to hesitate when remembering their past interactions. Hmmm…do you think maybe they… nah, probably just a technical glitch.

Having now established the overall workflow for my research project, I was finally ready to begin some live testing and begin capturing and processing some video footage to ensure the translation algorithm is working and make any necessary adjustments. Fortunately, with IBM Watson's amazing supercomputing capabilities I felt confident I would be able to create a process similar to the one I had used to study canine dreams, and which ultimately allowed me to establish actual two-way communication with the dogs in the study.

Attempting the same level of interaction with squirrels is a completely different story, especially since I would be collecting data live with subjects in the field. First, I will need to feed Watson as much video and audio data as he… I mean *it* will require in order to conduct a meaningful comparison to all available research into squirrel communication abilities and interactions. The objective will be to create a comprehensive data mapping matrix, a type of language translation utility, similar to that used by Google Translate and other translation applications. Of course, in this case the challenge is much more complex due to the fact we know squirrels communicate by a complex series of vocalizations, but also by using their tail position and movement, sort of like their own version of sign language with punctuation marks for inflection and emphasis. For this to work, the video I will be sending Watson will have been processed using a series of post-production applications, which will isolate each of the squirrels and track their movements, sounds and tail positioning. Hopefully, a sufficiently large amount of data and my translation algorithm will allow Watson to create a new squirrel "language" database.

The next step will then be to use the language translation utility to convert the individual squirrel "conversations" into an English translation a human (me) can understand. If I can accomplish that, I am confident we can then reverse engineer the process. Yes, I realize it's weird, but the plan is for me to use readily available technology to provide me with real-time translation during my observation of the squirrels and allow me to immediately respond in a language they will understand. Now, that is not to say I necessarily expect any conversation I might have with a bunch of squirrels to make any sense, but I need to at least give it a shot if I ever hope to understand what these diabolical varmints are up to.

During my observation and recording sessions in the park, whenever the entire group of squirrels were together and communicating, I had a hard time focusing on even just one or two, much less five or six. They were constantly chattering and scampering all over the place, seldom remaining stationary for more than a few seconds. That, plus the fact that their tails are flicking back and forth and, more importantly, the squirrels are not simply operating solely in one area or on one level. Just when I was able to lock in and visually track one animal, it would suddenly go vertical and do a 90 degree turn straight up a tree, disappear around the trunk of the tree, then reappear seconds later flying headfirst down the opposite side and dart across the ground. Watching this spectacle was like watching a three-ring circus, with half a dozen performers displaying various acrobatic feats at the same time. It's a good thing my camera was capturing it all, because my eyes and brain found it impossible to keep up.

In reviewing the edited video footage with the subject tracking application engaged, I was finally able to associate vocalizations with a specific squirrel, which then allowed me to begin to see reactions from the other subjects, sometimes seeming as though they were responding to one another. If that is in fact the case, I suppose it is quite possible I was observing an actual squirrel "conversation", but without the benefit of further analysis, that is purely speculation, hallucination, or possibly both. Now that Watson has had the opportunity to analyze the edited video, a comparison to ALL published studies of ALL squirrel species from ALL sources in ALL countries should allow the creation of a comprehensive data matrix with the potential to match specific vocalizations, tail movements and other observable behavior nuances to responses and behaviors of other members of each observed group.

Assuming I can access Watson's full artificial intelligence capabilities and can then use the research meta-analysis to identify communication patterns and apply my translation algorithm, we may be able to create a rudimentary type of language "dictionary" we can then use to decipher squirrel communication, similar to cracking an unbreakable secret code. In considering the complexity of such an undertaking, it also occurred to me the task is further complicated by the need to assign unique identifiers to each of our subjects. In doing so, would we also need to consider the sex, age or other characteristics of every subject squirrel? OMG!

At this point there was really only one way to determine whether the process I had envisioned would have any real potential for success. It was time to return to the park and give it a shot.

Nine

Ready for Testing

I watched a squirrel fall from a rather high branch. Upon hitting the ground, he bounced slightly, paused, shook himself vigorously and then immediately scampered back up to the very same place on the very same branch from which he'd fallen. There are some that might call that stupidity. Then there are others like myself who would call that tenacity. And while I generally have no interest in being a squirrel, in this particular respect I wouldn't mind being like one.

~ Craig D. Lounsbrough

When my iPhone alarm chirped at 6AM, I laid in bed for a few minutes contemplating the game plan, and I smiled when I stopped to realize I was actually looking forward to the day. Remembering to place a cup under the coffee maker for a change, I jotted down a few notes and double-checked my equipment list. This would be the first time I would be using the Amazon Alexa mobile app to provide a direct interface to Watson and, provided T-Mobile cooperates and can handle the additional bandwidth required for what is sure to be massive data transfer, Alexa should allow me to use hands-free voice commands to direct what will either be a magnificent symphony or a completely disastrous shit show.

On the way to the community park, I was pretty psyched-up, like the hormonal rush you get just before a sports competition. I am no athlete, but as a scientist I have trained for this challenge. In anticipation of what I hope to achieve in this initial session, I found myself both anxious and excited as I ran through the intricate maze of complex interactions that would be required, from the equipment to processing the vast amount of data I hoped to collect. During the drive I pictured an optimum scenario and imagined a successful outcome, which would eventually lead to actual communication, such as the breakthrough I was able to accomplish with my previous canine study. If I could achieve anything close to those results, just imagine! For a moment, I pictured myself presenting at the prestigious *Animal Conversations* conference in Stockholm. When the attendees hear the results of my research and the implications of my findings regarding squirrel motivation, imagine the looks on their faces when I... Wait! What is...

Something distracted me for just a split second. I am frankly not exactly sure what it was, but I sensed motion – something I could not quite identify, although whatever it was seemed to be in the road ahead, moving from right to left. I suppose my reflexes must have taken over in an effort to avoid whatever it was. To be perfectly honest, I am not clear what happened at this point. I know I was almost to the park, and later was told my car veered off the roadway, jumped the curb, and slammed into a small oak tree on the park perimeter near the street. Daydreaming, or more accurately – *drivedreaming* has its consequences. Apparently the airbag deployed – thank God for that – and a short burst from the horn on impact startled a neighbor watering her petunias. Honestly, I can't say my life flashed before my eyes or anything so melodramatic, but I faintly recall what felt like a spinning sensation and a weird mixture of noises – tires skidding, brakes squealing, thumping vibrations, then complete silence. I am still a bit fuzzy on the details, but I do remember coming to my senses (at least I thought so at the time) and I was able to open the car door to exit the vehicle.

I heard my neighbor running toward me shouting "Hey! Are you OK?"

"Yeh, I think so, thanks."

"Are you sure? You're bleeding."

"Yeh, I'll be f…" I couldn't quite complete "fine", before doing what would later be described as a truly world class face-plant into the recently watered grass surrounding the base of the tree.

I remember waking up, slowly opening my eyes, trying to maneuver my hand to brush away the leaves and dirt immediately in front of my forehead. As I raised my head, my fingers found my face, and I could see blood apparently emanating from just above my nose, most likely from the airbag impact. I could hear my neighbor on her phone with the 911 dispatch operator, and she assured me help was on the way. Looking straight ahead, I saw a blurry gray blob maybe 6-8 feet in front of me… no, make that *two* gray blobs – not blurry, *furry*! There were two gray squirrels intently observing my current embarrassing predicament. Now, this is where… OK, I know this sounds weird, maybe a little crazy, but *I swear I clearly heard them talking*. No, I didn't say I heard them making squeaks, chirps, and clicks. I heard them *talking*. No shit! It was brief, but their little mouths were moving, and tails were shaking like crazy. I heard them clearly.

"Dude hit the ground pretty hard. You think he's dead?"

"Nah, look. See? His eyes are blinkin'."

"True, he's bleeding, though. He don't look too good."

"They *never* look good, bro."

I glanced over as my neighbor walked over to check on me, and I could hear sirens in the distance. When I looked back, the squirrels were gone. I tried to raise my head again and wanted to stand up, but she cautioned me:

"No, no! Just relax. The paramedics will be here in just a minute. Lie still."

"But I just heard…" That's the last thing I remember – lights out.

I regained consciousness (or at least thought I had) when I slowly opened my eyes to a blinding white light. No, it was not a portal to heaven or… Turns out it was precisely what it seemed, a bright light from the paramedic's flashlight checking my responsiveness.

"Sir, can you hear me?"

I struggled to focus, squinting from the light in my eyes and eventually honed in on a shiny object, which I determined was the name tag on my would-be rescuer. It's funny how the brain works. I was lying on the ground just a few blocks from my home, realizing I was in an auto accident. I could feel the damp grass on my legs, hear the noise of the blood pressure cuff on my arm and felt its slow release, but I was laser-focused on a shiny object engraved with the name "Carl Johnson". For some unknown reason I felt compelled to recite it, perhaps to demonstrate my reading ability – hell, I don't know why. It just seemed like the thing to do.

So, I proudly and quite emphatically proclaimed: "Carl Johnson."

"*There* you are! That's right, sir." Carl had a big grin; he probably appreciated the formal recognition. "That's me. Me and my partner here – we're sure glad you're OK. Looks like you had a minor accident, but the air bag did a number on you."

"Air bag? Accident?"

"That's right. When you stepped out of the car, it looks like the impact from the air bag caught up with you, and you hit the ground. Lucky it's just grass!"

"Lucky… Yeh, lucky I guess."

"Sir, I think it's probably just a slight concussion, but as a precaution we'd like to transport you so the ER can run a couple of tests. Is that OK with you?"

"Hospital… Yeh, no problem. Thank you. I need to let my wife know."

"Your neighbor here just spoke with her, and she will meet us there."

Now, to be clear and perfectly honest, I have absolutely no clue what the neighbor's name was/is, but I could see her standing behind the paramedics and talking on the phone as they helped me on my feet and onto the ambulance stretcher, so I smiled, gave her an awkward thumbs up and mouthed "thank you". I may never know her name, but of course I won't forget my new buddy, Carl. Just life, I guess.

The stretcher wheels wobbled as they left the grass and transitioned to the paved sidewalk, and I could hear the ambulance communications radio blaring from the nearby street as we approached. But I also heard voices in the background and turned in a vain attempt to locate the source.

"Dude! They got him strapped in on that cart thing."
"I'm seein' it. I ain't blind, ya' know."
"Look at the car, bro! Won't see that one again for a while!"
"True, true. Good thing for us. One less."

As I was being loaded into the ambulance, I heard what sounded like high-pitched giggling, like a bunch of mischievous children. I remember thinking "That's weird", since I couldn't see anyone else, but I *definitely* saw my car, which faired much worse than its more substantial oak tree adversary.

At the hospital, I was checked for any signs of physical injury, asked an endless series of questions, checked for cognitive function and responsiveness, given a CT scan and admitted for observation. As I was wheeled into my room, I was greeted by my wife, and her face said it all, an odd mosaic of concern, support, bewilderment, with a smidgen of evil-eye thrown in for good measure. Don't get me wrong, I could tell she was clearly concerned and wanted to make sure I was OK.

That was really not in question. But once she was able to cognitively process the fact that I was alive and likely to remain so, well…I knew what was coming. At that instant I felt like a child who was just caught with his hand in the cookie jar. In fact, it's a good thing they weren't checking my blood pressure at that point.

As she took in the scene of me in a hospital gown, hooked up to an IV drip and monitor, she leaned in and planted a kiss on my forehead.

"How are you feeling?" It's the most obvious, supportive, and nonconfrontational question.

"I'm fine. It's nothing, really. Just one of those things."

She smiled and nodded. "Yes, things happen."

"The car… airbag…" I stammered, looking for evidence to support my assertions.

"Yes, Harriet called and told me. I stopped by the park on the way here. I saw the car. You're a lucky guy."

I realize I should have been thinking "You're right; I am very lucky it wasn't much worse." But for some reason I may never fully comprehend, my brain somehow got stuck, mired in processing the word "Harriet". I'm wondering "Who the hell is Harriet, and what was she calling about?" Thankfully, my diminished cognition and mental hiccup cleared sufficiently for me to at least attempt to fake it.

"Yes, Harriet saw the whole thing and called 9-1-1. I'm lucky she was there."

Have you ever watched someone's facial expression transition from concern to curiosity? You know, when you can clearly see they have completely processed the conversation up to this point, are ready to speak and move on, and are only waiting for your response to end so they may continue the interrogation…er, uh, I mean *conversation*.

"It looked like you must have swerved and jumped the curb?"

"Yes, I tried to…" She continued before I could complete my sentence.

"Tried to avoid that oak tree?" Oh boy, here we go! She shook her head. "Looks like that didn't work out."

"Yes, but…" I tried to get in a few words, but no luck.

"Let's see…it was cloudy this morning, so no sun glare issues."

I felt my stomach tighten. Or maybe it was my sphincter. Maybe both.

"It was early, and you don't drink, so… Hmmm." She continued: "Your phone would have been on Apple Carplay, and it doesn't look like you were on a call or texting, so not a case of distracted driving." She held my phone in her hand as if to let me know she had checked it thoroughly.

Is it hot in here? I swear the hospital room was freezing just a minute ago. So why am I sweating? She continued:

"Must be a mechanical issue. Steering linkage, perhaps?"

Crap! I was watching a skilled prosecutor carve up a defendant like a skilled hunter field-dressing a wild animal.

"Well, I was coming around the curve – not fast at all, but something…"

"Something moved out into the road? An oak tree? They are sneaky… and fast!"

"No, it…"

"A neighbor backing out of their driveway?"

"No, it wasn't…"

"I know! I've got it. It was those damn kids on the golf cart. I'm surprised they were up that early."

"No, it wasn't that. It was…"

"It was what, honey? What caused you to swerve, jump the curb, and wrap our brand new EV around a poor innocent oak tree."

"Just as I was coming around the corner, they ran out into the road right in front of me. What was I supposed to do?" I implored her to consider the gravity of the situation. She wasn't having it.

"Now, honey…when you say 'they', who are you referring to, exactly?"

"It was…it was, you know…"

"Actually no, I *don't* know. Can you please solve this vexing mystery for me?"

"It was a bunch of squirrels."

Unable to withstand the pressure of the interrogation, I succumbed and blurted it out, instantly regretting it. It was a moment of involuntary reflex honesty. Imagining the continued, increasing browbeating and likely waterboarding that lay ahead, I broke. You've seen it in movies and the famous line "Eventually, they *all* break." Me, I'm a complete wimp. The second I said it I wanted to take it back, but too late - my response had already entered the space-time continuum and the auditory wave vibration began its slow-motion journey from my lips to her waiting ears just a few feet away.

When my response reached its destination, the impact was immediately visible. First, a simple twitch, as might be triggered by an electric shock. I then observed the head complete what appeared to be a 360° exorcist-style rotation, coming to rest as her widening eyes sent out tractor beams to latch onto mine, forcing them open to meet her gaze. This beautiful love of my life, somehow transformed into a highly trained CIA interrogator dominatrix at this secret black site hospital room.

"Squirrels? Did you say (pause for dramatic effect) *squirrels*?" Aw, shit! Here we go!
"I was just driving, looking straight ahead, I swear. They came out of nowhere. There were at least three of 'em. They were right in the middle of the road. I hit the brakes and…"

"Is that when the squirrels pointed toward the oak tree?"

"No, they didn't..."

"They didn't erect a barricade or post a *Squirrels Working* sign suggesting you should leave the roadway?"

"No, of course not. I just... it's just instinct, I guess. I didn't want to..."

"What? You didn't want to make pavement pancakes? You'd prefer scrambled car? What a lovely choice!"

"I wasn't thinking about..."

"Yes, you *weren't* thinking! You could have been killed!" At this point I could see she was upset (duh!) and was beginning to get emotional. She came closer and grabbed my hand. I put mine over hers to console her; it's what husbands do.

"I know, sweetie. I know. I'm sorry. I would... hey, ouch! My hand! Shit! Ow, that hurts!"

Fortunately, at the pinnacle of my formal torture, admonishment, and evisceration, the doctor arrived to share the results of the tests and my prognosis. My wife and I listened intently, although I noticed she would not let go of my hand, probably just in case she heard something she didn't like. Apparently I suffered a slight concussion from the airbag deployment and a small cut on my forehead that bled a lot, but aside from some minor scrapes and grass stains, I would most likely survive. Of course, it's a bit disconcerting to hear a doctor proclaim: "Good news! We did a complete scan of your brain and found nothing." I was too embarrassed to have him check my recent hand injury.

I was discharged the same day. The doctor prescribed rest and no physical exertion or driving for a day or two, reminded me I would be quite sore for a while, and wrote a prescription for pain meds and a "sleep aid". If they were anything like whatever they put through my IV, *I would most definitely fill that script!*

Well, I guess the drugs must have done their job, because I only vaguely remember leaving the hospital, but I realized when I was finally at home in my own bed that I was one lucky guy. Surviving the incident gave me a renewed sense of purpose, and I was determined to immediately get back out there and complete the field testing. For now, I was still a little woozy and just wanted to get some rest.

Ten

Close Encounters of the Squirrel Kind

> Did the squirrel realize how lucky he was to be there? Or on the contrary did he spend his life wondering whether he might not be better off somewhere else, or feeling that he didn't have the life he deserved? In the end, it depended on the comparisons the squirrel was able to make.

> *~ François Lelord*

Yesterday was a disaster, and once I was finally able to relax at home in my own bed and pop a couple of my pain meds and a "sleep aid" with a glass of wine, I drifted off into some much-needed sleep, well before my typical bedtime. It didn't take long to enter REM (rapid eye movement) sleep, the stage during which most dreams occur, and this was no exception. You may recall a large part of my clinical research, especially over the past several years, has been dedicated to studying how humans and animals sleep and dream. Our groundbreaking research findings in the *Dog Dreams* study focused specifically on the canine brain's activity during REM sleep and dreaming. In case you may be unaware, REM sleep comprises about 25% of your total sleep cycle. During REM sleep, your brain activity actually looks very similar to that when you are awake.

For me, I have found that when I sleep, and especially when I dream, I often find myself imagining where my current research might lead, sort of seeding my dreams with a real-life challenge. Then when I wake up in the morning, I realize I spent a good portion of my REM dream phase plotting various scenarios for the day's activities. Yes, I realize that sounds like a major nerdfest and waste of valuable dream time, but I guess it's just the way I am wired. Tonight especially, following such a horrible field study failure, automobile accident, and possible auditory hallucination, I guess my brain was determined to try to get things back on track. So it was not surprising that when I reached that blissful but active REM stage, my dreams took on the challenge of planning a more successful outcome for the day ahead.

Having made substantial progress with my translation utility, and thanks in large part to the teamwork of Alexa and Watson, coupled with Watson's incredible processing speed and artificial intelligence capabilities, I finally felt I was ready to field-test the technology. This warrants a brief reminder and recap of the process, with a goal of establishing a real-time interaction with one of the squirrels. For the proposed "dialogue" to occur, I will be capturing a live video stream from my iPhone with audio from a parabolic microphone, processing it through a series of post-production applications to isolate an individual squirrel and its associated vocalizations, then transmitting the processed digital feed using the Alexa mobile app to IBM's Watson. Watson will analyze the video and compare it to the extensive research data library to match the vocalizations, behaviors, and tail movements and their resulting responses from other squirrels, then use my translation algorithm to convert that output to audio using a sophisticated AI speech synthesizer. Whoa! What a mouthful!

Then comes the really tricky part. Watson will be processing and returning data to me almost simultaneously in real-time and will be expecting my immediate verbal response. That will require my meager, limited human brain to listen to what the squirrel is "saying" and instantly offer a response. Reversing the process when I respond verbally, the Alexa app will transmit the data to Watson to use the translation utility to create a synthesized audio response vocalization in a "language" the squirrel will understand. That audio will be played through a loudspeaker array aimed in the general direction of the subject squirrel. Now, if you don't think that is just about the most complex and seemingly insurmountable challenge you have ever heard, then... well... Just trust me on this one, will you?

During my previous visits to the community park for observation and recording sessions, I initially had a hard time following the group of 5 or 6 squirrels that frequented a small clearing near a fence line separating the park from an adjacent homeowner's yard. There was simply so much going on at the same time, it was difficult to isolate just one or two of the squirrels, especially when they were darting about or chasing each other across the grass and up into the surrounding trees. But after I became accustomed to the location and was more comfortable with my recording equipment, I started to notice that a few key players stood out from the others, and for completely different reasons. One was what I eventually confirmed to be a male squirrel that was especially energetic and seemed to be constantly in communication with the others with almost constant vocalizations and tail signaling. The other was an obviously older squirrel and, while I could not determine the sex, the subject was nowhere near as active as the others, choosing instead to remain in the shade of an oak tree. This squirrel seldom vocalized, except when one of the others invaded its personal space by passing too close and apparently annoying the squirrel in question. Only then did the subject seemed to be "chewing out" any squirrel that ventured too close, like a "don't poke the squirrel" type scenario. After some thought, and since the older squirrel was less communicative, I decided to concentrate my efforts on the other more active and vocal subject.

I must have run through what I imagined to be a first contact scenario at least a hundred times, including in my dreams, working through what I anticipated to be possible outcomes. These included every conceivable dimension, from overwhelming immediate success to abject failure and rejection, realizing of course that the most likely result would land somewhere in the middle of that spectrum. My imaginary run-throughs gave me a certain degree of confidence that my research, planning, preparation, and process had at least a reasonable chance of actually working, but I admit I approached this first attempt with considerable trepidation. In any research project, there is always that moment of truth when we test a theory through a field trial, and… well, as they say: *there is no time like the present.*

For me, my heart was close to leaving my chest, but this was no time for anything other than a calm, professional demeanor. Tripping over an exposed tree root and almost falling on my face as I turned to move toward the clearing was not the most graceful approach, but I was able to regain my footing and move to a position that allowed a clear, unobstructed view of the field of play. I moved slowly but deliberately, as this was the first time I was moving into view and no longer concealed behind what had become my clandestine bush hideout. I moved the tripod with the iPhone and parabolic microphone mount into position and checked the phone screen to make sure I had the area properly framed before activating the live feed. I slipped on my Bluetooth headset. It's showtime!

"Alexa, please alert Watson we are ready to go live."
No response. Hmmm…That's odd!

"Alexa, I am in position and ready to go live. Please alert Watson to activate the translation utility." Silence.

"Alexa?" Nothing. Nada.

I reminded myself that, while both Alexa and Watson should be expecting my instructions, fully prepared to respond, the weak link might well be something as simple as cell signal coverage. Shit! Come on, T Mobile! My phone signal was showing four bars. What the hell?

"Alexa? Alexa, are you there?" At this point I was getting concerned.

As my voice grew louder, the squirrel I had identified as my initial target, S2, had already noticed me and was standing erect with his tail fully upright, twitching occasionally as if to alert the others, but with no vocalization. I was momentarily convinced the squirrel was staring straight at me, no doubt curious about my intentions. After a short, awkward silence, S2 dropped to all four paws on the ground, alternating in and agitated back and forth motion and barking in a high-pitched tone, with his tail twitching constantly and waving upright like a signal flag. I remained motionless, glancing at the phone screen out of the corner of my eye to make sure the camera was capturing the action. The squirrels responded to S2's vocalizations with their own barks, clicks and squeaks and tails going every which way, but none retreated and one, S1, remained in the same spot, seemingly oblivious to the commotion created by the others. S1, by the way, was the label designation assigned by the tracking software to the older and less active squirrel I mentioned previously, and I had guessed the #1 designation was because the subject's lack of movement made it the first the software could easily isolate, label and track. In any event, as I remained very still, the group soon accepted that I was not a threat and returned to foraging and other normal squirrel behavior.

Slowly taking a step forward, I was now standing at the edge of the clearing, fully exposed. Wait, check that. I mean… I wasn't *exposing myself* to the squirrels, rather I had fully revealed myself and was completely visible to the group. Just as I was about to try to connect with Alexa again, S2 began to move in my direction, seemingly unphased by my presence.

Trust me, what happened next…well, I never imagined. I was standing there with my iPhone in my hand and was just about to try Alexa again, when S2 scampered over to a tree stump only a few feet in front of me, then stood upright and looked me straight in the eye.

"Hey, you've been eyeballin' me for a while. What's up?"

Holy shit! There was a squirrel right in front of my face talking to me! I was dumbfounded and temporarily paralyzed, unable to respond. I can't imagine the astonished, shocked look on my face, but I'm pretty sure it was a doozy.

I was completely bewildered and trying to process what was happening. The right side of my brain was telling me that what I thought I had experienced as I laid on the ground following the accident had *actually happened.* I could feel the euphoria of validation as I flashed back to that moment as I first regained consciousness on the grass. But almost instantly, my left-brain synapses were firing, pulsating much like raid fire punches in the face, letting me know in no uncertain terms that I was quite clearly delusional and should immediately seek psychiatric care. Cognitive dissonance then followed as the result of my brain's vain attempt to resolve the simultaneous conundrum and paradox. I will spare you the psychobabble; in layman's terms: *I was in deep shit.*

Meanwhile, back at the stump… the squirrel was no-doubt carefully assessing what was unfolding in front of it, which included a human with a complete dumb-shit look on his face, apparently either a mute, in shock, simply too stupid to be able to verbalize a response, or some combination of those options. This extended thought process had, of course, taken some time, and the squirrel had been waiting impatiently for a response. Since none was forthcoming, it apparently decided to take it up a notch.

"Hey buddy. You! Are you hard of hearing or sumpthin'? You doin' OK? You look like you're freakin'."

Well, I *was* freakin', so the squirrel had *that* right. At this point in the story, I need to pause to explain a minor nuance, a line we are about to cross, and that requires some clarification. You will notice when speaking about the encounter with the squirrel, at least up until now, I referred to the squirrel as "it", clearly avoiding any anthropomorphic attribution to the animal. That creates somewhat of a conundrum, because for the first time I have now *heard* the squirrel speak. Notwithstanding the fact that may well make me quite insane (I might concur with my own self-diagnosis), I heard the voice of a *male* animal. Granted, I could disregard this as irrelevant for the purpose of my scientific study, however there is one problem with that approach. The squirrel in question was on a tree stump less than three feet from me. Further, *it was standing upright*. If you haven't gotten the picture by now, let me help you out. The squirrel has a penis and testicles and has now spoken to me with a distinctively male voice. We could quibble over my description of the attributes that comprise a *male* voice, but for the sake of time I ask that you trust my skilled professional judgement on this one. In the absence of a formal request regarding preferred pronouns, this squirrel will hereinafter be referred to as a *he*. Lest we keep *him* waiting…

"I'm sorry. It's just that I wasn't expecting you to speak." I stammered nervously.

The squirrel – you know, the one we just established was a *he*, cocked his head and recoiled in disbelief.

"You weren't *what*? You thought we would just stand here and stare at each other? By the way, buddy, my eyes are up here." His paws pointed to his eyes, most likely because he saw me staring directly at his balls, purely as I continued to confirm his sex…for my research, of course.

"Sorry, I didn't realize squirrels could talk."

Oh, shit! I knew that was stupid. What was I thinking? Looks like I pissed him off. Yep, never thought I'd see a squirrel with such an incredulous look, but I knew I had really stepped in it. He spoke:

"Well, that's odd. I thought you came out here specifically to talk to us." At this point I could see the other squirrels moving closer, and they were seemingly eavesdropping on our conversation and intently observing the interaction.

The question, of course, was whether I was prepared for the conversation and real-life *Doctor Doolittle* scene that was about to unfold.

Eleven

The Conversation

If we had a keen vision of all that is ordinary
in human life, it would be like hearing the grass
grow or the squirrel's heartbeat, and we should
die of that roar which is the other side of silence.

~ George Eliot

Looking back, I can't imagine a more improbable setting than what was unfolding right in front of my eyes. Here I was in a small community park with lovely grass, flowers, trees, and shrubs and – oh, did I forget to mention? Squirrels! An epic battle scene is set. A drone's-eye view of the landscape below reveals a research psychologist (that's me, by the way) with a substantial array of now completely non-operational audio, video and communications gear positioned on one side of an oak tree stump. On the other side, a group of maybe 5 or 6 common gray squirrels, one of which is current standing upright on the aforementioned stump, having thrown down the gauntlet in a brazen challenge to the dominion of the human adversary. This was clearly looking like the apocalypse, an epic *squirrelmageddon*. Overly dramatic? Sorry.

I suppose some might view the scene as preparation for an attack. That *did* occur to me, and I admit the thought of a pack of wild, possibly rabid squirrels launching an attack on oh, I don't know…*MY FACE* did rattle me more than just a little. In retrospect I guess I envisioned the situation more as an alien invasion - you know, the whole "take me to your leader" thing. Only in this case, it is hard to cast the squirrels as the alien invaders. In fact, maybe the roles are completely reversed, and *I'm* the one invading *their* world, about to meet *their* leader. Yep – let's go with that.

Of course, looking back now it is easy to pretend I was able to process all of this while standing in a park face-to-face with the possible squirrel king, or whatever title might apply in this case. Shit! Should I begin my introduction with a bow or formal salutation? Hell, the entire fate of human civilization might well hang in the balance. This could upset the delicate ecological hierarchy, the one where we somehow see ourselves at the top of the food chain and evolutionary ladder. So much to think about! After some reflection and a few deep breaths, I decided to keep it informal, at least to start.

"Hey, how are you? Yes, I did come here to observe you guys. I live here in the neighborhood, and I'm doing some research."

"Research? Wait! Are you that psychologist, the one who wrote that book…?" Holy shit! The squirrel kept talking, but my brain jammed at the word "book". Are you kidding me? *This squirrel knows I wrote a book?* How the hell could he possibly know that?

"Yes, that's me. But how did you know that?" My face must have been grotesquely contorted with such a puzzled look!

"Simple, Doc. I saw your picture on the back cover." What? I can't possibly imagine the complete dumbass look on my face. This had to be a joke, right? Somebody is obviously pranking me big-time. I did a quick scan of the area looking for hidden cameras, only to realize I was the only one who brought any. This squirrel recognized me from a picture on the back cover of a book about dreaming dogs, and I'm supposed to act that this is just a normal conversation between strangers?

"Well, uh…I, uh… yeh, I was here doing some research trying to learn about squirrels."

"Well, you've come to the right place!" The other squirrels made sounds that clearly sounded like suppressed laughter, the kind you might make when you think it best to figure out what's going on before you risk totally losing it and laughing out loud – you know the feeling.

"Nice to meet you, Doc. Can I call you Doc? You're a doctor, right?

"Not exactly, I'm a research scientist, a clinical psychologist. I have always been fascinated by squirrels, so I came here to learn more about the squirrels in our community." See what I did there? Pretty sly, huh? A little flattery, indicate interest… If only I had some nuts, I would have them eating out of the palm of my hand. What? Too much? Fine, back to the story…

"You want to learn about *us*?" Giggling, clicks, and squeaks, with lots of tail waving gyrations. The squirrel continued: "No problem, Doc. What would you like to know?"

Let me pause here to explain what you are no doubt already wondering: do squirrels have names? During the course of my research on squirrels as previously noted, and as soon became apparent later during numerous reconnaissance sessions in the neighborhood park, squirrels communicate among themselves using a variety of gestures and mannerisms, such as flicking their tails one way or another. They "speak" to each other though certain postures and vocalizations, recognizing each other visually, but also through their keen sense of smell, something I am unable to measure and document in the current project. As a result, each animal very clearly knows the others, so labels and formal names are not necessary. Since, as a human, I lack any such uncanny ability to distinguish one from another, at this point I really needed them to have names! I realize that may seem selfish and presumptuous, but it is, quite simply, the only way I could ever keep them all straight and properly relate this story.

"Well, I guess I was wondering if squirrels have names, and if so, what's yours?" At this point the squirrel cocked his head, dropped to all four paws, and moved toward me, stopping just inches away, directly in front of me, returning to a standing, upright position on his back legs. It was not a menacing move but frankly, it made me a bit nervous.

"I am Sam." he said, extending his right paw. Now keep in mind, I am not a tall guy, but at 5 ft 10, let's just say I had to bend down quite a bit to shake hands… I mean *paws*.

"Very nice to meet you, Sam" I exclaimed as I grasped Sam's paw and took a moment to process the entire scene. The smile on my face came from an overwhelming sense of wonderment, like I was in some fanciful Disney-esque animated feature film.

"Sam, you seem to know about me and why I am here, and I would love to hear more about you and your friends." Feeling more relaxed, I decided the best way to continue our conversation was if I sat cross-legged on the grass near the paved walkway. Even in this position I still loomed large above the squirrels, but Sam seemed to appreciate the effort and moved up onto the stump as if to meet me halfway.

As Sam and I were settling in to begin our conversation, the other squirrels seemed to become more inquisitive, eager to eavesdrop on our discussion and curious about my presence in the park now that my cover was blown. One squirrel in particular, a female, moved in close behind Sam as he spoke. Sensing the movement, Sam turned to acknowledge her, and I could not quite hear their brief exchange. When Sam turned back toward me, at the same time he motioned for the female squirrel to move forward and motioned for her to stand next to him. Hmmm…something was up!

"Doc, I would like to introduce you to my partner, Samantha." Aha! Now I understood! Samantha seemed hesitant and shy, understandable given the current circumstances. As she was introduced, she glanced in my direction, then maneuvered her way in my direction, just in front of Sam.

I smiled and bent down, offering my hand. "It's nice to meet you, Samantha. I know this is all a bit much, and I look forward to learning more about your species." Crap! What the hell did I just say? *Species?* Really? That sounded awfully cold and scientific, like I was referring to a bunch of lab rats. Wait a minute! I guess that actually *does* accurately describe what I was doing there.

"It is nice to meet you, doctor." Samantha showed a toothy grin I took as a smile. Frankly, it is hard to tell when a squirrel is smiling or simply the pronounced overbite. Regardless, I smiled back as Sam returned to our conversation, but just as he was about to speak, Samantha unexpectedly and nervously blurted out:

"I want you to know I am enjoying your book." I was stunned! Oh my God! She knows about my book! How could that be?

"You…you're reading my book? I am so flattered! How in the world did you hear about it? Do you have…are there *squirrel* book stores? Did you order through Amazon? Wait, how would the driver know where to deliver? How did you get it?" I was peppering this poor squirrel with questions! Sam stared at Samantha, or maybe *glared* is a better description.

Samantha moved closer and answered: "Actually, *you* delivered it." A sly smile on her face told me there was more to come. "When you were here in the park last week spying on us, you left a copy on the picnic table." She cocked her head inquisitively, waiting for my reaction.

Hmmm…thinking back, I wondered what happened to that copy. That explains it.

"Yes, I remember. You must have taken it while I was packing up my equipment. Pretty sneaky!" I was smiling and nodding, not wanting to seem too accusatory.

"I must admit I did take it, but I just have to say it has been delightful!"

Wow! I felt a sense of pride and accomplishment. It is always gratifying to hear positive comments about my work, even when they are coming from a squirrel!

"No offense, but I didn't know squirrels could *read*."

Oh my god! It was as though I had ignited an explosion! The entire group (reminder: a group of squirrels is called a "scurry") erupted in loud, uncontrollable, raucous laughter. No, not just a few snickers, chuckles, giggles, and guffaws! I'm talking ear-popping, rip-roaring, side-splitting, hysterical belly laughter. Did I mention incessant? These little rodents are having a psychotic meltdown right in front of my eyes, and the cacophony of uncontrolled laughter is really starting to piss me off! The scene looked like a sort of squirrel rave, constantly pulsating, jerking, trance-dancing – tails flipping all over the place, little squirrel paws raisin' the roof – you get the picture. Everything but pills and vaping – I didn't see any of that. I guess they know better.

I gathered my wits, took a deep breath, and held up my arms to signal I wanted to say something. I didn't want to be "that guy" or come off as aloof and unappreciative, but all I could muster were the words to appropriately express what you are no doubt wondering right now.

"Hey, what is so damn funny?"

Samantha emerged from the still pulsating scurry. As she approached me, I knelt down in a sort of haphazard genuflection, and I could see she was trying her best to catch her breath, control her own laughter, and compose herself. As the others saw Samantha moving in my direction, the noise level slowly subsided, with sporadic cackling outbursts punctuating the moment. Trying unsuccessfully to gather her wits, she alternated between covering her mouth with her paws and averting her eyes, looking down and away from my face, now just inches away. And then she looked up and said:

"*Read*? You didn't know we could *read*?" As she emphasized the final word, the group again erupted into complete pandemonium, and we were off to the races again! Wait! What the heck is going on here?

After what seemed like an eternity and quite possibly out of sheer exhaustion, the noise level began to subside. From her position in such close proximity, Samantha could see in my face a combination of bewilderment, embarrassment and anger.

She quietly and gently explained: "No, Doc. I wasn't *reading* the book. The pages make perfect *nesting material*."

The scurry immediately erupted again, descending into new depths of raucous depravity. What the hell is wrong with these guys?

Twelve

Introductions

It's like a cliché, but true, that writing is
intensely solitary and at times really lonely.
I sit in one room and talk to squirrels and
blue jays all day.

~ Douglas Coupland

Have you ever suffered an ultimate embarrassment?
You know, like loudly ripping an excruciatingly
odiferous fart in a small group setting, with no way to
possibly avoid responsibility? Or maybe that terrifying
microsecond when you realize your finger hit "send" on
a text to the wrong person *that was about the wrong
person*? Shit! In my case the situation was made even
more devastating by the fact that my entire professional
existence had just been completely obliterated by a
squirrel. A freakin' *talking squirrel*!

Sensing my extreme embarrassment, Samantha
retreated slightly. As she moved back beside Sam, I saw
a young squirrel peering out from behind them. It
appeared to be an infant, and I could not determine its
age or sex, but I could clearly see it belonged to Sam and

Samantha, no doubt about it. I moved slightly in an attempt to get a better view of the little one, only to immediately find myself caught in a game of peek-a-boo with the baby (here in the South some call it *peep eye*). In an effort to break from this cute but unwinnable contest, I looked back at Sam and Samantha with a question.

"And who is this cute baby? Boy or girl?" Oops, I should have thought about that one! Shit! What if squirrels also have several genders? Preferred pronouns?

Samantha immediately offered: "It's a boy."

"That's wonderful, congratulations! What is his name?"

Sam jumped in: "We call him *Baby*."

Hmmm...I'm thinking: OK - simple, straightforward. But at the same time, I couldn't help but wonder how that's going to work when he goes to squirrel school... Wait a minute! No, don't get ahead of yourself.

"Hello, Baby. Nice to meet you." I smiled as Sam motioned for Samantha to showcase the youngster. Apparently, in an effort to somehow acknowledge the greeting and involve Baby in the recognition, Samantha picked him up, all to the delight of the group. On closer inspection, I could see that Baby had a large acorn in his mouth, with the stem protruding, acting as a sort of pacifier. As the infant squirmed in her arms, Samantha grabbed the acorn with her paw, plucking it from Baby's mouth and creating a sound similar to a cork popping from a bottle.

Now, all I can say is that this simple act triggered an eruption similar in magnitude to Mount Vesuvius, St. Helens – hell, whatever *mount* conjures your worst possible version of a tremendous, violent, and unrelenting outburst. The sound can best be described as something like a combination bloodcurdling, ear-splitting yet low-pitched, agonizing scream, like the voice of Satan during an exorcism, together with an air raid siren, but SO much louder. I heard my sunglass lens crack and suspect any fine crystal in nearby homes likely suffered a similar fate. Afraid my ear drums would burst, from my awkward cross-legged position I leaned over, put my head between my knees, and attempted unsuccessfully to shield my ears. I felt dizzy and feared I might succumb and black out. Suffice it to say, it was not something easily forgotten.

Before I could vocalize my extreme distress, Samantha returned the acorn pacifier, stuffing in the little squirrel-of-a-bitch's pie hole, nut hole, whatever hole his little mouth needed filling to shut the hell up! Suddenly, the auditory onslaught subsided, the ground no longer trembled, tsunami warnings were lifted, and I was able to regain my composure once again… sort of.

Sam was completely embarrassed, as Samantha offered a brief and timid one word apology: "Sorry!" She retreated, Baby in tow, and settled in the shade of a nearby bush.

At this point I do have to note that when Sam introduced me to Samantha, there was something about the look in his eye that told me she was more than just his "partner". Over the course of my research and in observing Samantha in her interaction with Sam and other members of the group, I found Samantha to be the most interesting of the identified research subjects. Let me explain.

In Florida and most other southeastern habitats, gray squirrels typically have two litters of 2-4 babies, with one litter in the first few months of the year and another in the summer. As with several other mammal species, newborn squirrels are blind and remain to nurse with their mother for more than a month before venturing out on their own in 3-4 months. I mention these facts to call attention to the fact that Samantha is, in my expert opinion, a truly amazing example of a multitasking mother, teacher, protector and warrior. She is a mashup of just about any female Marvel or other superhero and whoever you consider the undisputed world's best mom, whether that may be your own or an inspiration - someone you hold in especially high regard. If you do the math, and allowing for courtship, mating, and gestation, that effectively means Samantha is "available" for other squirrel duties, including the types of roadway and other missions in question, just 2-3 months during the year.

I turned back to Sam, who was still shaking his head in disbelief and smiled as I said "So, where were we?" Sam shook his head and laughed.
"Now that I've met your partner and Baby, I am interested in learning more about *you*."

At this point, my interest was not false flattery. It seems every group has a leader, and that is at least somewhat true for squirrels, as well. The difference, as I learned from my research, is that squirrels are by their nature, independent creatures. Gray squirrels may choose to live in community groups in proximity to other squirrels but most generally prefer to live alone. They do, however possess excellent communication skills, which include sharing information regarding everything from the location of food sources to warning of predators and other potential dangers. As I was researching gray squirrel behavior, I found that while each squirrel may choose to act independent of the group, when they are called to action, they unite and assume their assigned role to support the mission of the team. In those cases, someone – oops, I mean some squirrel must take the lead in coordinating an activity, and that is certainly of utmost importance when darting out into the road in front of oncoming cars. In our case, that squirrel is Sam.

Sam might best be described as that reluctant and unassuming team member that emerges in situations that require at least a modicum of direction to keep things moving in order to achieve an objective. For the purposes of my research and in an effort to provide the scientific data I hope to use to convince these devious creatures to refrain from challenging unsuspecting drivers, I recognized early on I would need someone… damn! I would need a *squirrel* to interface with the others and that would be especially important in this case – well, you know – the fact I'm not a squirrel and all. The more I can learn about Sam, the better chance I will have at convincing the group to stop their dangerous roadway behavior.

I watched as Sam returned to his upright position for his stump speech (sorry, I couldn't resist…), and he began sharing his background.

"Well, the short version is that I was born and raised right here in this park. My dad left when I was just about Baby's age. My mom said he was hitting the nut juice pretty heavy, and he was never around much, anyway. He was always a tail chaser and ran off with some low-branch floozy. My mom took it pretty hard, but she's a strong sow. (That's what female squirrels are called, by the way.) My grandfather trained me right over there in that oak tree. I must have busted my ass a hundred times! It seemed so much bigger back then. He's getting pretty old now and has some issues, so I stepped up to help with the scurry."

As luck would have it, while I was in the middle of my "conversation" with Sam, one of my neighbors approached from the street on the walkway. I didn't recognize her and turned briefly in her direction as I was speaking so she could see my Bluetooth headset, indicating I must be on a phone call. That was certainly one plausible explanation for a man standing facing a clearing in a neighborhood park and talking out loud, the other being schizophrenia or worse. I suppose I could have simply stopped to explain I was talking to the squirrels, but I doubt she would buy the truth in this case. Fortunately, she smiled and nodded as she passed by and continued down the walkway, but that meant she might possibly return at some point.

As I turned back to continue the conversation with Sam, I could see he had been watching my reaction to the neighbor with interest, or perhaps he was just annoyed that I had interrupted him in the middle of telling me his story. I apologized for the interruption and returned to my position facing Sam and the other squirrels.

"Sorry again for the interruption. That was one of my neighbors."

Sam nodded and immediately responded: "Yes, I know. She lives in the green house on the corner, the one with the two oak trees in the back. She has an amazing bird feeder, but she doesn't keep it filled. Her mate likes to tinker with squirrel-proofing things, at least he *thinks* that's what he is doing. Putting grease on the feeder pole? Really? Pretty *old school*."

Wow! That was interesting! How could Sam have that kind of information, even about her husband? I had to ask.

"Really? You seem to know a lot about my neighbor!"

"We make it our business to know things that are important to us. Oak trees are important; they have acorns. Access to bird feeders is important. Watching humans trying to deny us access…well, that is always *entertaining*."

"I guess I never thought about it that way."

"Maybe that is because you are the first human who has shown an interest. I mean, there *is* that one strange older female that lives next to the tennis court. She likes to sit in her backyard near her flower garden and tries to get us to come up on the arm of her chair to feed us by hand."

I smiled. "Well, that's nice of her, isn't it?"

"You call that *nice*? I don't think so. First of all, *we don't really know her*. She feeds *all* the animals – birds, rabbits, deer – you name it. She even feeds pigeons. Pigeons! That's just *gross*!"

"Well, I'm sure she means well. I don't really know her personally, but…"

Sam interrupted: "Exactly! We don't know her, either, but a friend of Samantha's visited there frequently. One day she just disappeared; we never saw her again."

Ouch! That was pretty sinister and a little spooky. I always wondered about that barbeque pit...

"I'm getting a little uncomfortable...Can we get back to what we were talking about?"

"You mean, *about me*?" Sam shook his head, and his tail relaxed, curling around his hind paws as he sat back. It was as though he was settling in, hopefully feeling more comfortable with my presence.

"Yes, I am here to learn more about you and your group. So, you are the leader of the scurry?"

"I don't know about *leader*. I guess I am more like a *coach*, a *player*-coach. I try to keep everyone organized as a team, and we all do our parts to contribute. I can't *make* any squirrel do anything. We just all agree on what needs to be done, and I help make sure it happens."

"So there is no formal hierarchy or authority? You don't see yourself as being *in charge*?"

"No, it doesn't work that way. We are too busy trying to just survive, feed our families, raise our kits."

"Wait, did you say "kids"?

"No, our babies are called *kits* – some say *kittens*. And before you say anything, yes – I know that's what you call young cats. We don't much care for cats." When Sam said the word "cats", Baby squirmed, squealing loudly, forcing Samantha to hold the acorn pacifier firmly in place. As Sam was speaking, I jotted down some notes, excited I was actually gaining useful information, precisely the purpose of my research.

"I can certainly understand that. I am sure there are many threats you have to deal with."

Sam nodded in agreement. "And that's why we focus on what is important *to us*. Knowing if you humans have a pet - that's important. Knowing if you have children, especially young boys with BB guns, bows and arrows, or slingshots – that's important to us. Knowing which of you drive fast – that's important to us." I nodded and held up my hand to signal I got the message.

"I understand. I do." I had to pause for a moment to reflect on what was happening.

Regardless of how Sam chose to describe his role, I quickly realized I was having a conversation with the leader of this scurry of squirrels and was starting to look at things from a completely different perspective. No, I was not able to fully comprehend or see things through their eyes – at least not yet, but I was beginning to see that I would have to spend more time getting to know about each squirrel and their role in how the group functions as the team Sam was describing.

Thirteen

Artemis

Living is no laughing matter: you must live with
great seriousness, like a squirrel for example –
I mean without looking for something beyond
and above living, I mean living must be your
whole occupation.

~ Nazim Hikmet

As Sam continued talking about his scurry, out of the corner of my eye I noticed one of the squirrels had positioned itself in the shade of an adjacent viburnum hedge and was intently watching our interaction, but it seemed to be constantly fidgeting and angling for a better vantage point. When I asked Sam, he laughed and responded: "Oh, that's my grandfather, Artemis." He smiled as he explained that Artemis was now essentially the equivalent of a chairman emeritus, a designation much like we might ascribe to a now senior citizen who previously held a position of power and importance. Sam shared that Artemis was in fact the leader of the scurry for many years and grudgingly stepped aside and surrendered his position only due to his age and health issues.

When I first met Artemis, I suppose I expected the squirrel version of The Godfather, the patriarchal head of this rag-tag band of squirrel commandos, like a commanding General overseeing an elite unit of well-trained special forces preparing to engage oncoming enemy vehicles. What I found was anything but that. Here was a *very* old squirrel, whose shriveled, weathered face looked like a parched desert in desperate need of a good rain. Of course, we are talking about gray squirrels, so naturally I anticipated the light, ashen coloration, but this was not at all the type of commanding presence or former squirrel king I had expected.

According to Sam, Artemis is more than 12 years old, which in and of itself means he is clearly in record-setting territory for the longest ever recorded squirrel life span in the wild. Of course, a quiet suburban Central Florida community may not seem like "the wild", but in most areas and due to environmental factors and the presence of predators, the life expectancy for a gray squirrel at birth is just 1-2 years, and the average life span of an adult squirrel is only about 6 years. By my calculation, which has absolutely no basis in scientific fact, Artemis is the equivalent of 114 years old in human years. You get the idea – *he is <u>really</u> freakin' old*! Let's just say that the candles cost more than the cake, if you know what I mean.

Unfortunately, Artemis' advanced age makes him a target for squirrels in other scurries in the neighborhood, especially the Millennials and Gen Z males. While Sam's close-knit extended family are protective of Artemis, respectful of his age and position, and are aware of his limitations and crotchety disposition, the same cannot be said of occasional disrespectful intruders, whose constant taunts are designed to rile up the poor old guy. Often when the squirrels in Sam's scurry are out early in the morning, the young thugs come around just to see if they can get a rise out of poor Artemis.

"Hey, old squirrel! I heard you're so old, your social security number is 1."

"Artemis – over here! Is it true when you were young rainbows were in black and white?"

"Dude! He's so old, when he was born, the Dead Sea was only sick."

"Dude, I heard your birth certificate was written in Roman numerals."

Sharing another example, Sam told me he recently overheard a conversation between Artemis and two other old squirrels sitting on a park bench and knew their hearing wasn't what it used to be.

"Windy, isn't it?"

"No, it's Thursday."

"Me too, let's go grab a drink."

Artemis claims that, as we often say about dogs, he may be too old to learn new tricks, but he insists that his old tricks still work just fine. As we were getting to know each other, he insisted he had a great joke for me, but when I offered to listen, he couldn't remember it. I nodded in support and assured him we all suffer from some degree of cognitive decline as we grow older. He managed a smile and responded:

"Well, you know what they say, the memory is the second thing to go."

I thought OK, I'll play. I asked: "Oh yeh? What's the first?"

He feigned confusion: "First *what*?"

During my conversation with Artemis and as geropsychologists often encounter, it was sometimes difficult to determine if his reactions were indicative of reduced cognitive capacity or rather simply a clever ploy to mess with a naive human intruder. As he shared the story of his early upbringing, I could swear I saw an animated twinkle in his eye, knowing I was hanging on his every word, waiting for the punchline that might or might not ever arrive.

I quickly learned Artemis is a great storyteller. The minute I asked him to tell me about himself, he immediately transformed into an elder orator holding court with me as his sole audience. Artemis grew up in the same park in my neighborhood, and he quickly made it clear he was talking about "way back in the day", which made me stop to consider what that phrase meant to an aging squirrel. If the life span of an adult gray squirrel is just 6 years, that fact adds considerable context to his view of his life history. In fact, I think it is fair to say that while Artemis is certainly the scurry's elder statesman, "back in the day" might include what we humans would consider fairly recent history. Regardless, his perspective on how things have changed in his lifetime offer a broader understanding of the species and speaks directly to the topic of my research.

Artemis recounted his early upbringing as the eldest son in a litter of four. He and his one brother and two sisters enjoyed the loving support of a strict father and caring, supportive mother. When asked about them, Artemis beamed with pride, explaining that his dad was a no-nonsense, strict disciplinarian, or as Artemis explained it:

"My daddy taught us about respect – for our elders, for sows (female squirrels), for the rules of the scurry. Papa didn't cotton much to young kits (squirrel children) who wouldn't listen, and I remember each and every time that disrespect included me! Oooee! He would light my squirrel ass up! Yes sir. Can't say I didn't deserve it."

I know it is neither professional nor scientific to speculate or read too much into facial expressions, intonation, and body language, especially in a species for which I have little knowledge. There was just something so genuine and loving in how he portrayed his upbringing, I found myself drawn in, hanging on his every word, and creating a mental image of his extended family.

"Yep, when I was out of line, which was more often as I grew older, my daddy would whoop the tar out of me. We didn't have 'time outs' back then. And if papa wasn't around, my mom would just give us a stern look and say: 'Just wait 'til your father gets home!' Heck, just thinkin' about it now makes my ass ache."

Artemis confessed that, as an adolescent, he could be a real handful and was known as both a prankster and quite the ladies' man.

"Yes sir, I admit I enjoyed a good prank – still do, if it's done right. I remember one time I was down by the pond and found a bunch of fishin' line with a lead weight and hook at the end. My best friend Calvin lived two trees over in a tree holler (hollow). Me and another squirrel, Tony, we climbed up outside that hole and sunk that hook in the tree bark real good on the back side where no one could see, leavin' the weight hangin'. We uncoiled the fishin' line down the tree and into a scrub palm where we could hide. We left it there until I got good and dark, so we knew Calvin would be sound asleep."

At this point I must have had a confused look on my face, which was immediately met with indignation and admonishment.

"Hold your horses, mister Doc! You'll see!" Oops, I guess he told *me*! Artemis continued the story.

"In the middle of the night, Tony and I snuck out and got that line, hiding underneath the scrub palm. Tony was the lookout, and I would pull that fishin' line back a bit, which pulled the lead weight away from the tree. Then every so often, I would let the line go completely slack, then pull it back again. You see what I was doin'? The weight would smack against the side of the hollowed-out spot in the tree, resonating on the inside where Calvin and his family were sound asleep. We'd wait to see if any heads poked out, wait a while, then pop that line again." I couldn't help but laugh.

"Oh my god, I get the picture! How long did you keep that up?" As I asked, Artemis grinned.

"If Calvin or his siblings poked their heads out, I would wait until everything got dead quiet, then light 'em up again. Can you imagine? Must have sounded like a woodpecker knockin'! Sometimes Calvin would poke his head out – even come all the way out, half asleep, and look around. Then I'd wait a while longer and do it all again."

I laughed out loud. "Now, that's just mean! Funny, for sure, but also *mean*."

"Yep, found that out the next day when Calvin's dad found the fishin' line and stopped by our nest. Guess I hadn't thought too much about the impact on others in Calvin's family."

"So what happened?"

"Well, long story short – Papa wasn't none too pleased. I got my ass lit up for that one. Made me go and apologize to Calvin's mom, and all."

"So, was it worth it?"

"Are you kiddin' me? Damn straight it was! Funny as hell! Guess you had to have been there."

Artemis went on to talk about his transition to adult squirrelhood, still at an early age, at least in squirrel terms. That twinkle in his eye I mentioned earlier? It seemed to take on a somewhat darker glow when he began to talk about his first sexual experience and the impact his promiscuity had on his psyche and overall personality.

"Yep, I remember the first time I ever had sex – remember it like it was yesterday. And I also remember sometime later when I did it with a sow (girl) for the first time." I covered my mouth to stifle the chuckle that was trying desperately to break through my fingers to become audible.

"Yeh, OK – I admit I was a tail chaser. Ya got me, there. Now, I'm not sayin' I was the most handsome squirrel around, but plenty of others were butt ugly and well, I got some moves, least I *had* some back in the day."

During this geriatric storytelling session, I watched closely as Artemis seemed to enjoy reminiscing and having someone like me express an interest in his long and eventful life.

"I realize now I was known as a *'love 'em and leave 'em'* type guy, kind of a *'wham bam, thank you m'am'*. I ain't proud of that, but I have to say I didn't mind it at the time. No, not at all." I watched as a wry smile appeared, and Artemis seemed to drift into a nostalgic daydream. I was almost scared to ask:

"Wow, how many *kits* (young squirrels) do you think all those encounters created?" In the back of my mind, I was thinking of potential human comparisons – *Nick Cannon* somehow came to mind.

"Hell, I have no idea, really. A bunch! I ain't proud of that, but I ain't ashamed, either."

Our conversation turned a bit more serious when I asked about the present, including Sam and the scurry. Artemis immediately became more animated and upbeat, offering his take on the current squirrel kingdom state of affairs and generally offering his opinion on the state of the squirrel world of today. Perhaps not surprisingly, there were immediate parallels to the current human condition.

> "I've gotta tell you, Doc. These young squirrels today…Heck, back in the day I would welcome the opportunity to learn from my papa. Sure, he was strict and maybe prone to overreact when he saw something that just wasn't right, but I sure wish there were more squirrels like that today. Since Sam's dad left him and his mom in a lurch, I tried to step in and help out whenever I could. I

can't take credit, but I think that boy turned out just fine. Shoot, young squirrels today... they don't appreciate how good they've got it, no sir. Talkin' back to their parents, stayin' out well after dark with all that's goin' on out there. It just ain't safe anymore. Sometimes you just wanna jerk their chain and slap 'em upside the head."

In an effort to steer the conversation to the members of the scurry, I tried to keep it open-ended.

"It seems like Sam and your scurry are doing pretty well." Simple, generic.

"Yep. Gotta hand it to Sam, there. He brings out the best in squirrels. Got his hands full with Baby, that's for sure. He's a real screamer, that one. Watch out – he's gonna be a real pistol. But the scurry, yeh, it's a motley crew, but don't let that fool ya. Darryl is smart as a tack, too smart for his britches sometimes, but a good team player. I've been workin' with Chad. Poor squirrel missed out on a lot, no dad and all. Nobody was there to show him the way, but you wait and see. He's kinda awkward, but he'll come around. Emma...now, that girl needs to be kept under control. The boys all say she's hot, but sometimes somebody just needs to snatch her up by the tail. She gets on her high horse and can be as windy as a sack full of farts. She doesn't understand the scurry comes first, and the world don't revolve around her prissy ass. If she wants to be a model, she can start by being a *model citizen*, if you know what I mean. Recently, since Samantha has her hands full with Baby, Mama has stepped in to let Emma know when she's actin' too big for her britches. Now, Rambo – that boy is a real piece of work! It's sure good having him around – kinda like having our own *Incredible Hulk*. I sure wouldn't wanna mess with him! Good news is he's *our* hulk." I found myself completely engrossed in the elder squirrel's snapshot summary of the group and wanted to wrap up the discussion by asking if, after reflecting on his own story, he had any words of wisdom for young squirrels today.

"Well, they've got plenty to learn, and I've got plenty to say, if they would just stop for a minute and listen. I tell them to make sure they never stop learnin', because life never stops teachin'. I heard somebody once said that the real tragedy of life is that we get old too soon and wise too late."

The more time I spent with Artemis, the more I realized the value of his generational knowledge and how it has positively impacted the group. My initial reaction was that he was very self-aware of his role in sharing knowledge with each member of the scurry and teaching youngsters such as Baby the requisite skills to survive in squirreldom today. And while his outward demeanor and often acerbic wit might come off as harsh and unfiltered, I think the old squirrel knows precisely what he is doing, even though the years may have taken a toll on him physically.

Somewhat stereotypically, Artemis exhibits many of the attributes one might expect from his elder human counterparts. His eyesight is failing, and his hearing has seriously deteriorated, a dangerous combination for a squirrel, which often depend on their quick reaction time to escape predators and avoid man-made dangers… like cars! Fortunately, Artemis has maintained an excellent sense of smell, which has allowed him to at least forage for nuts in a limited range within the fairly safe and well-protected community park, which abuts a larger heavily wooded undeveloped area. As I had the opportunity to observe and interact more with Artemis again later that afternoon, I quickly learned that he could be extremely ornery and combative, frequently chastising his younger counterparts and constantly sharing stories about how things were "back in the day". As Sam and I were talking, Artemis was preoccupied with some adolescent squirrels trying to impress him with their branch jumping skills, as they tried to maneuver toward the neighbor's bird feeder. I couldn't help but eavesdrop.

"You call that a challenge? Shit, back in my day I could scamper up that feeder pole with my eyes closed."

The young squirrels weren't buying it.

"Hey Artemis – why you wanna close your eyes going up a feeder pole? You gonna crack yo' head at the top!" The scurry immediately egged him on, much to the delight of the other squirrels, whose teeth chattering vocalizations I swear sounded quite similar to human laughter. As expected, that only served to rile up the old guy even more.

"Shut up, you squirrelofabitch! I ain't gonna crack bread nowhere! Ain't no bread up there most of the time – mostly just birdseed, if the damn crows didn't get there first."

Fourteen

Meeting Mama

The squirrel that you kill in jest, dies in earnest.

~ Henry David Thoreau

As Sam and I continued our discussion, I noticed one squirrel that had remained curiously stationary in the background, sitting upright under the shade of a small palm tree, seemingly interested in observing my interaction with Sam and the others. It was too far away to tell if it was male or female, but it remained virtually motionless except for what appeared to be wringing its hands, almost like washing or wiping them repeatedly. Watching it out of the corner of my eye, I finally asked Sam what was going on. He smiled, lowered and shook his head, and to my surprise announced:

"Oh, that's my mother. Everyone here calls her 'Mama'." I was completely taken aback! Thinking back to Sam's story about his upbringing, I knew his father was out of the picture, but he never said much about his mother.

"She likes to sit there in the shade and knit. Heck, she will do that all day when it's not too hot."

"Wow, I look forward to meeting her. She's *knitting*? What, getting ready for the harsh Florida winter?" I asked jokingly. As with so many other awkward, lame comments, it didn't occur to me that these squirrels had absolutely no point of reference for a world outside of this small residential community, so that joke would have bombed, regardless.

"She is actually really good at making blankets and sweaters, that sort of thing, mostly for Baby. The palm tree 'fur' we like to use for our nests can make some nice, soft padding."

I was listening to Sam and now intently watching his mother as he shared more of the story of his upbringing. When Sam's father ran off with a younger female, his mother was understandably pissed off, but she was careful to hide her anger and resentment from young Sam, choosing instead to make sure he had a proper upbringing, including involving Artemis as a well-respected role model for the young squirrel. Sam said he was sure Mama was well aware that the relationship benefited Artemis, as well, as he was getting older and enjoyed reliving his younger years through helping Sam learn everything a male squirrel absolutely must know, if you know what I mean. Based on the way Sam spoke of his mom, I could clearly sense the love and respect he had for Mama.

Later, as my conversation with Sam continued into the early afternoon, he eventually waved and motioned to let Mama know he would like her to make her way to our position at the tree stump so he could properly introduce her. I could see her putting away her knitting and watched as she moved across the lawn with a unmistakable, distinguished sense of style and grace. As she approached the tree stump, Sam extended his paw to guide her, a perfect gentleman greeting his mother with great respect and politeness.

"Doc, I would like to introduce my mother. Everyone calls her 'Mama'. Mama, this is… this is 'Doc'."

I bent down and extended my hand. "It's a pleasure to meet you, m'am."

Extending her paw, she glanced down demurely: "Just call me Mama, young man. Everyone else does. So, I understand you're a doctor?"

The scene was quire surreal, and I felt as if I was being introduced to a royal matriarch. Here was a middle-aged female squirrel, looking like she came from the cover of a glamour magazine. Every hair in place, tail perfectly coiffed, with a certain air about her that seemed somehow familiar.

"Thank you, Mama. Actually, I am a research psychologist working on a project studying squirrel behavior, but feel free to call me 'Doc'. Sam has been kind enough to tell me a little about his upbringing. He certainly sings your praises."

"Well, bless his pea-pickin' little heart! He's a sweet boy but not much of a singer. I don't think he could carry a tune if he had a bucket with a lid on it!"

I chuckled and attempted to restrain busting out a belly laugh, which caused Sam to furrow his brow and give me a mean side-eye. I was thinking "Good one, Mama!" but certainly wouldn't say it out loud.

Now, I know this sounds weird and no, it's not my imagination. I swear Mama squirrel *has a Southern accent!* I know that doesn't make any sense at all, and I'm pretty sure I'm not completely crazy, but the minute she opened her mouth I was completely dumbstruck. How could this be? I was having an acute attack of self-diagnosed cognitive dissonance! In case you are not familiar, in psychology, cognitive dissonance is the mental discomfort people feel when they realize their thoughts and actions are inconsistent or contradictory. She *couldn't* have a Southern accent; that doesn't make sense. *I know that.* But my ears definitely *heard* it. My brain clearly processed it. How could that possibly...? I caught myself in mid-thought; neither does the fact that she is *talking*, you idiot! What the hell is going on here?

Regaining my composure, I gave Sam a supportive nod, before continuing.

"Mama, Sam told me a little bit about himself. I wonder if you would mind doing the same?

"Well, there's really not much to tell. Thanks to my no-good husband running off with that squnt, I was left with nothing but baby Sam and my knitting needles."

I wasn't sure what a "squnt" was exactly - possibly some type of derogatory squirrel contraction?

"Yes, m'am. Sam told me about that. I am so sorry to hear that."

"It's not *you* who should be sorry. He was as worthless as tits on a bull - lower than a snake's belly. He thought the sun comes up every day just to hear him crow. He took everything he could carry and ran off with that cheap floozy. She was acting so high and mighty, her nose so high in the air she could drown in a rainstorm - always wearing that cheap perfume he found in the dumpster next to the pond. You could smell her all over hell's half acre. I shouldn't say it, but word is she's spread out like a cold supper." Mama turned up her nose in disgust, visibly agitated.

"That must have been devastating." I didn't really know what else to say.

"I don't know what he saw in her except they both liked to party, but one day he just never came home. Last I heard they were living under an old pizza box a few streets over, not even a proper nest."

I could almost feel the emotion and anguish and almost wished I hadn't asked, but Mama continued.

"Sorry, there I go pitchin' a hissy fit! Where are my manners? You were asking about our story, and the truth is, sometimes it wasn't pretty. We had nothing. Heck, we were so poor we couldn't afford to pay *attention*." Where in the world does she come up with these zingers?

"Well, it sure looks like you were able to raise a very capable young squirrel."

"Thank God he's not like his daddy! His grandpa surely did make a man out of him, bless his heart."

As we continued our conversation, I asked about her interests and learned that Mama was an excellent cook, and apparently her recipes are widely regarded and shared in the squirrel world. I suppose the closest parallel would be that she is like the *Paula Deen* of the squirrel culinary universe, with a flair for foraging for the freshest ingredients and coming up with unique seasonal creations. One thing I found fascinating was when I first heard others in the group extolling the virtues of Mama's *baked goods*. While you are *digesting* that fact (sorry), please pause to consider the implications of that seemingly innocuous comment. *Baked goods!* Just how the hell can a squirrel, even one with exceptional culinary training and experience, *bake* anything? Have you seen any squirrel ovens or air fryers advertised recently? Is this all just a bunch of hot air? OK, I will stop, but I knew there must be more to the story.

Mama explained that her "oven" was actually a one-of-a-kind invention courtesy of Darryl, a member of the scurry you will meet later and who is, by all accounts, quite the squirrel genius. Mama said she originally got the idea from a young child in the neighborhood during the summer, when she would set up a lemonade stand. Apparently the child entrepreneur chose a location curbside next to the community's tennis court, which serviced both walk-up and drive-thru customers. The young girl and her mom cheated on the lemonade, using a Country Time powdered mix for the brew, with a fresh lemon slice helping sell the impostor beverage as fresh-made. In addition to traffic from thirsty tennis and pickleball players, what really attracted neighborhood customers was an assortment of fresh baked cookies. As Mama explained, it was really the cookies that were the draw, with the lemonade simply something to wash down the mostly dry, crumbly treats. As was typically the case with any food products within smelling distance of the scurry's community park headquarters and following all festivities held in the park itself, the squirrels would be sure to scavenge through the area, looking for any leftovers and crumbs they could find. In the case of the cookie/lemonade stand, Mama was always first in line at closing time, having watched from a nearby tree branch.

Fortunately, the young girl was a kind soul and loved seeing Mama perched nearby. Before tearing down the setup for the day, the child would try to entice Mama to come closer, offering small pieces, crumbs, and even an entire cookie. Over the course of a few days of the same scene playing out, Mama simply could not resist the temptation, and slowly but surely got close enough to snatch a tasty snack, much to the delight of the young girl. Even better, Mama realized that at least some of the cookies had one ingredient no self-respecting squirrel could resist – nuts! Always the polite and caring matriarch, Mama would bring back anything she could carry to the other members of the group. Samantha and especially Baby gave the delicious snacks two paws up (squirrels don't have thumbs), and Mama was bound and determined to learn more about the source of this tasty *nut nirvana*. The next day after the stand closed for the day, Mama followed the girl home to a house adjacent to the tennis court and pond. The following morning, she returned to the house and hopped up on the flower box outside the kitchen, which offered a perfect window vantage point. She watched the girl and her mother preparing cookies – mixing the ingredients, *which often included nuts!* Mama took note of every move – the ingredients, mixing, putting small spoons of batter on cookie sheets. But wait! Then the metal cookie sheet trays would disappear into a mysterious cave in the space below some type of contraption where things were bubbling in pots and pans above. Where in the world did they go? The girl and her mother left the kitchen and disappeared into another room. What the heck? What is going on here?

Returning to the scurry, Mama shared what she had seen with Samantha and Emma, who were disturbed to hear of the unexplained cookie disappearance. Whenever the word "cookie" was uttered, Baby would howl and flail his arms, as though demanding answers to the vexing mystery. Overhearing the discussion, Darryl passed by, offering a one-word response: *oven*. Mama and Samantha immediately snapped their heads around in unison, demanding "Wait, what?" Darryl returned with a bit of geekspeak, explaining that an oven is a very hot box that "bakes" things, including cookies. That succinct explanation was, of course, immediately met with more howling and arm flailing, followed by an excruciatingly loud and foul-smelling Baby fart. What followed was a lengthy discussion during which Darryl experienced some type of unexplained savant epiphany, one of those "light bulb" idea moments, the result of which was a strictly theoretical methodology for creating a type of solar oven.

Sparing the technical jargon, the plan Darryl developed would direct famously abundant Florida sunshine through a lens Darryl fashioned from a badly cracked concave glass bowl left in a trash receptacle in the park following a community event. Darryl demonstrated the concept to Mama and Samantha by propping the cracked bowl up on an adjacent fence and angling it to capture and concentrate the sun's rays, acting like a large magnifying glass. As the rising sun moved into perfect alignment, the result was a highly concentrated beam so intense it caused the pile of leaves on the ground below to catch fire before the panicked squirrels frantically stomped it out. Darryl smiled, then further explained a plan to create a simple box-like structure using stones and mud for mortar. Then the glass would be positioned to concentrate the beam on the rocks, which would quickly heat and hold the high temperature, creating the world's first squirrel oven and making it abundantly clear this was an oven *created by squirrels* and not meant *to bake them*! All that remained was selecting a spot within the community park area, away from the walkway, well out of sight, and with no obstructions to block exposure to the sun throughout the day. Once completed, Mama immediately set about experimenting with all sorts of nutty recipes. I imagined I would be hearing more about her progress soon.

As I had the opportunity to observe and interact with Mama more, I could see she was a huge help to Samantha with both Baby and Emma, Samantha's oldest, each in very different ways. For Baby, Mama was the proud and nurturing grandmother figure, while with Emma she filled the role of intermediary, acting as a buffer when Samantha and Emma got into it during their mother vs. adolescent spats. Mama's calm but firm no-nonsense approach will be important in supporting both the mother and often rebellious female.

Fifteen

Rambo? Seriously?

I've started collecting taxidermy:
I've got a red squirrel, called Steve.
I made sure he came with certificates, so
we know he wasn't just killed for stuffing.

~ Arthur Darvil

S am introduced me to a squirrel named Rambo, a moniker I initially found odd, at least until I learned more about him and his role in the scurry. As Sam made the introduction, a larger and mature male squirrel stepped forward, and offered a crisp salute before extending his paw to shake hands. To properly set the scene, when I use the term "larger", keep in mind that we are still talking about a squirrel as compared to a human, in this case *me*. When standing erect, Rambo is maybe an inch or two taller than Sam and clearly stands out, dwarfing the others in the group but, of course, I am reaching *way* down to reach his outstretched paw. I should also note that when shaking hands with a squirrel, the whole *paw/hand* clasp is not exactly equivalent, such that the "shake" is between the squirrel's complete paw-hand and maybe a finger or two of mine. I mention all of this because, unlike my initial introduction to Sam, Rambo grasped my index and middle fingers in an especially firm, some might say *aggressive*, way. In fact, a more accurate adjective might be *excruciating*. What the hell? This super-rodent was squeezing the shit out of my fingers! Watching the blood drain and color change from flesh tone to white, our eyes locked just long enough to let me know I did not want to eff around with this guy. Determined not to cry out, I was able to momentarily maintain my composure long enough to stammer "Nice to meet you" before the vise grip was released.

"Good to meet you, sir." Rambo's voice was deep and resonant, somewhere on the continuum of James Earl Jones, Morgan Freeman – maybe more like Trace Adkins.

As I was regaining the blood flow and feeling in my hand, Sam introduced Rambo as being "in charge of security" for the scurry and mentioned he helped coordinate "missions", which he said he would explain in more detail later. I'm thinkin': "Damn, who the hell is going to mess with *this* guy?" Partly in an effort to allow me to step back and draw attention away from my behind-the-back hand wringing, I tried to lighten the mood with an obvious question.

"Wow, Rambo! That's a cool name. You know, we have several movies…" Sam interrupted mid-sentence.

"Yes, I think we've seen them all."

I recoiled in disbelief, thinking: What? Are you serious? I watched as Rambo and the others nodded in agreement.

"But…how did you? How could you? I don't…" My confused babbling just sort of trailed off.

"Caught 'em on *Nutflix*. I think we binged the first three in one night. Watched the others just after they came out - once they made it to streaming."

Just as I was about to seek clarification on the *how on earth squirrels are able to consume digital media* issue, Sam continued to explain Rambo's role in the group, and he began with a story. Apparently Rambo came to the group as an orphan, and no one knew exactly what happened to his parents, other than rumors suggesting they met an untimely fate when their nest was raided by a bobcat. Regardless of the verisimilitude of the story, Sam's scurry took the young squirrel into the clan and raised him as they would their own. He was an awkward youngster, mostly due to his size, dwarfing the other members of the group, even as an adolescent.

When he wasn't helping with food gathering or other chores, Rambo spent his time working out and was frequently seen lifting objects that exceeded his own body weight – tree limbs and logs, huge stones, and legend has it he lifted both rear wheels of a child's tricycle left unattended in the playground within the park. As a result, his muscular build soon lived up to his namesake, and the other squirrels came to view him as a protector warrior, always vigilant and unafraid. That role was tested one night when an intruder was detected, and squirrels on the lower branches of a large oak tree sounded the alarm. As the clicks and squeaks reached Rambo's hyper-sensitive ears, he immediately ran directly into the attack only to find an unimaginable terrifying adversary, a bobcat! Perhaps it was because he had heard the stories of how his parents were taken in the night when he was just a pup, but the squirrels who witnessed the ensuing battle swear they saw Rambo leap across multiple branches to create the first line of defense directly in front of the nest, as the cat stealthily approached. The resulting face-to-face stare-down must have puzzled the large feline, who was not used to such a standoff and expecting an easy, unopposed victory.

Squirrel witnesses peering out from inside the nest were terrified. How could one squirrel, even one of Rambo's size and strength, possibly withstand the imminent attack? As the cat crept closer, like a lioness stalking its prey on the Serengeti, Rambo locked eyes and focused on the bobcat's rear legs, watching for even the slightest tightening. He knew those muscles would flex first and signal the start of the forward pounce. In the exact instant that trigger revealed itself, Rambo matched it, first with a deep squat. Then, as the cat leapt forward, Rambo sprang directly upward, his vertical leap clearing both the bobcat's front claws and snarling jaws, causing the cat's face to plow into the twigs and branches that comprised the outer protective ring of the nest. Shocked, disoriented, and spitting out twigs and leaves, the cat hissed loudly, only to find that Rambo had dropped directly onto its back, just at the neckline. Firmly grasping and twisting a pawful of cat fur, Rambo rode the cat like a professional saddle bronc rider, refusing to let go as the bobcat bucked and shrieked loudly. Rambo used his razor-sharp incisors to sink deep into the cat's ear, which caused it to lose its footing on the branch and fall to the ground below, as Rambo released his grip, bailed out, and took up a position on a lower branch. During the encounter, the entire scurry was yelling vociferously, so much so an adjacent homeowner turned on his outdoor security lights, flooding the park with a blinding beam, sending the cat running full tilt down the path toward the woods.

Rambo is the GI Joe, special operations squirrel commando that sees every scurry undertaking through the eyes of a tough-as-nails combatant, completely unafraid and charging into battle recognizing this mission might possibly be his last. In fact, as I was able to observe and learn more about him, and speaking strictly as a trained psychological professional, to put it in layman's terms: Rambo scares the shit out of me.

Sam shared an incident from the week after the 4th of July when Rambo returned to the scurry's squirrel camp headquarters with a bunch of leftover fireworks some neighborhood kids had left in the nearby cul-de-sac, suggesting during the pre-mission briefing he would "use the unexploded ordinance to create improvised explosive devices to create a distraction." I can only hope you now share my concern that Rambo envisions himself to be the leader of a sort of *Squirrel Team Six*, and unsuspecting folks like you and I are his Osama bin Laden, unsuspecting enemy combatants, and potential battlefield casualties as a result of simply trying to get safely home. He is a lethal squirrel mashup of *Rambo*, *Winter Soldier*, and *The Punisher* and every bit as pissed off as *John Wick* – you know, right after the bad guys killed his dog. Trust me, you really don't want to get in his way.

I did learn, however, that Rambo's escapades were not always focused on search and destroy missions. One particular incident caught my attention, and in thinking back, I had actually heard about it several months earlier through our community newsletter. A young boy was riding his bicycle in the neighborhood, not an unusual occurrence on a sunny Saturday afternoon. As he returned home and rounded the corner of his driveway, the bike skidded in some sand and gravel, and he hit the pavement hard. With his left foot pinned beneath the bike and unable to free himself, all he could do was call out for help, but no one was around to hear his cry. No one except a courageous squirrel. Rambo and the test of the scurry heard the child yelling, and Rambo immediately ran toward the disturbance. Quickly evaluating the situation, Rambo moved underneath the center of the bike frame and pushed, and pushed, groaning and summoning all of the strength his small but muscular frame could muster. Push…higher…more…almost there! Once the bike frame was tilted sufficiently, the boy was able to extricate his foot and roll out of the way, as Rambo lower the bike to the ground. The relieved child lay motionless for a moment, catching his breath and slowly checking his injuries, fortunately limited to a sprained ankle. Still flat on the pavement, turning his head to the side he found himself face to face with his squirrel first responder and rescuer.

The story did not end there, however. As the young boy struggled to get up on his feet using the bike for leverage, he limped slowly to his front door, occasionally glancing back at Rambo, who had been joined by others from the group. The child watched in amazement at the excited squirrels exchanging high-fours with Rambo and creating a ruckus he could not quite make out. Greeted by his mother at the front door with a reassuring hug, the boy began a rapid-fire description of what had occurred. Urging his mom to look toward the street, he quickly realized the squirrels were nowhere to be seen.

If that sounds like a sweet story ending, my more thorough research on the incident revealed that the boy continued to repeat the story to other family members, friends, and his schoolmates, tragically resulting in mockery, humiliation, and embarrassment. At school his completely truthful, accurate, and detailed account of the incident was brought to the attention of the child's math teacher, who alerted the school nurse and counselor, who in turn recommended the poor kid visit a mental health professional. Following an initial evaluation session and a battery of psychological tests, the boy was diagnosed with acute Delusional Disorder, successfully completed a regimen of cognitive behavioral therapy (CBT), and was prescribed anti-psychotic medication. He no longer rides his bike in the neighborhood and has reportedly suffers from myoclonic seizures triggered whenever he sees or hears the word "squirrel" – a sad ending, indeed.

Returning to Rambo, while the bicycle rescue incident clearly shows he may be well-intentioned, to say he is a little over the top in preparing for the squirrels' typical activities is probably the world's greatest understatement. If you think for a minute I am exaggerating, take for example the fact that, unlike the other squirrels, before a mission Rambo darkens his normally white squirrel underbelly and the area immediately between his eyes and nose whiskers with his own special combination of asphalt road tar and dark potting soil he collected from an adjacent homeowner's flower garden. During the squirrel mission planning sessions which I was allowed to observe later, Rambo explained his pre-mission ritual and that his warpaint mixture meant "They'll never see me comin'!"

While you are no-doubt trying to somehow reassure yourself that sounds like a perfectly rational explanation, he would then work himself into an almost religious fervor, with a persona I would describe as akin to Hulk Hogan. Sam explained that he ultimately had to counsel Rambo to calm down whenever the issue of "roadway incursions" came up. Apparently Rambo envisions cars moving down the street as combat vehicles – tanks, Humvees and the like, designating humans as enemy combatants. Sam shared an incident in which he overheard Rambo talking to some young squirrels from a nearby scurry, treating them much like a drill sergeant would challenge recruits going into basic training.

"This is WAR, squirrel brothers! Dart quickly and stand firm until you see the panicked look in their eyes! Dash til' they crash! Are you with me?"

At that point, Rambo would raise his tail straight in the air with his extremely muscular squirrel arms fully outstretched, while the others would join in with the chant "Dash 'til they crash! Dash 'til they crash!" Hey, wait! Don't *YOU* start!

On a positive note, Rambo's strong persona and towering presence seems to bring comfort and a feeling of security to the group, with the squirrels always staying within close proximity of one another, allowing them to react quickly to any real or perceived threat. I also noted that what they lack in terms of the communication devices we humans depend on every minute of the day, the squirrels make up for with their incessant, distinct, and complex vocalizations and tail gestures, allowing them to maintain constant contact with each other. Unfortunately for me, I could not exactly run all of that visual communications input through *Google Translate* or look to hire a squirrel sign language interpreter from a listing on job posting sites or social media listings. At least I felt quite comfortable that Rambo was a great protector to have around.

Sixteen

Darryl

Eatin' squirrel brains is where ya get your smarts.

~ Miss Kay (Duck Dynasty)

I don't suppose I ever expected to hang out with a bunch of squirrels and soon realize there is always a nerd in any group. (Yes, I realize that just sounded like hanging out with a bunch of squirrels is not, by itself, unusual.) For this group, that description fits Darryl perfectly. When Sam introduced me to Darryl, I immediately observed his shy, timid demeanor, choosing to remain apart from the others to fulfill his extraordinary contribution to the team. He is more or less the group's logistician, and I later learned he uses his apparently exceptional advanced mathematical skills to provide the calculations necessary to allow the squirrels to surprise and outmaneuver the unsuspecting human drivers. To describe Darryl and his unique set of skills, the best analogy I can offer is the genius character in *Good Will Hunting* combined with *A Beautiful Mind*, in this case the mind of a squirrel. If you happen to be a fan of virtually *any* television series dealing with spies, CIA, FBI, MI6, special ops or anything remotely related to supporting secret agents in the field, there is always that one genius character that operates out of the home base and handles the behind-the-scenes brain power and technology. In this case, that is most definitely Darryl except, of course, the fact squirrels don't possess the elaborate headquarters, supercomputers, state of the art sophisticated communications equipment, and futuristic weaponry.

According to reports, Darryl is somewhat of a mathematical genius, able to make lightning-fast calculations and solve complex problems involving spatial geometry and an understanding of applied physics. In fact, he may well be a squirrel savant, especially considering the fact he was nest-schooled and essentially self-taught. It is hard for me to imagine that what we refer to as *savant syndrome* in humans might also apply to squirrels, but it could certainly explain Darryl's incredible skills across multiple disciplines. In humans, savants typically are preoccupied to obsession with specific facts relative to things like music, memorization of all sorts of trivia, historical dates, and facts, and may possess extraordinary abilities like those Darryl has exhibited. I found it fascinating that one rather odd obsession is his uncanny memorization and cataloguing of detailed motor vehicle specifications. In other words, Darryl is a car nut! Oops! These darn nut references are hard to shake!

Sam explained that Darryl's role in the scurry was to provide "research and logistical support for our missions." Initially I wasn't sure what that meant, exactly, but after having an opportunity to observe his participation in the group's activities, this dude is pretty remarkable. Of course, that begs the question: how in the world has a *squirrel* version of *Rain Man* been able to master such complex and intricate processes without the benefit of the years of education and training we humans have the opportunity to experience? My suspicion was that Darryl's brain may have a parietal lobe with a more highly developed pre-frontal cortex, the complex left-brain network, which in humans controls our mathematical ability and problem-solving. If I could just get him to sit still for a functional magnetic resonance imaging scan (fMRI) - man, that would be… oops, sorry! I'm getting a little ahead of myself.

I was so intrigued with the reports on Darryl's abilities, I felt compelled to at least follow up with a one-on-one interview in hopes of understanding more about how such incredible intellect found its way into the brain of a gray squirrel in my community. I mean – what are the odds that I would be doing research on squirrels and have a savant miraculously appear? Uncanny! Damn, I should have bought a lottery ticket! Before I had an opportunity to directly observe Darryl in action, as Sam had described his responsibilities, I asked Sam if it would be OK for me to meet with Darryl to collect some basic information and run a few cognitive tests. Yes, I realize it sounds weird, but I theorized that if Darryl's capabilities were anywhere near as amazing as had been reported, he might respond to the same types of testing instruments we use for human subjects. Sam discussed the idea with Darryl, and he agreed without hesitation.

It's a bit unusual to meet with a research subject outdoors in a park under a tree, but since having me attempt to climb up…well, that just wouldn't work. I sat cross-legged on the grass and extending my hand as Darryl found me on the far side of the park, well away from the rest of the scurry and out of view of adjacent neighbors. Surprisingly, Darryl did not appear at all nervous, but rather seemed intrigued at the prospect of participating in testing. As I would typically do with human subjects, I began by asking him to tell me a bit about himself and his early squirrelhood. Often, having a subject highlight his or her early upbringing may provide useful clues to aid in the evaluation. Darryl described what I suppose would be considered a fairly typical squirrel family environment. His parents were always around, and both participated in nest-schooling and early squirrelhood development with Darryl and his brother and sister from the same litter. According to Darryl, his first memory of anything noticeably different from his brother and sister came from what became his obsession with creating various mechanical inventions. A noteworthy example was what can best be described as a kind of rudimentary tricycle. Apparently Darryl had observed young children riding tricycles and bicycles in the cul-de-sac near the park. He immediately grasped the general concept and function of the wheel, considered requirements for steering, and immediately set about fashioning a squirrel-sized version using screw-top lids and an assortment of scrap metal and wire collected on days just prior to neighborhood trash can pick-up. He explained that he started with a tricycle after watching so many kids falling over trying to learn to ride bicycles. That fact in and of itself provides insight into Darryl's ability to process his observations into a vision for plans for iterative prototypes, taking in new information and learning each step of the way. He smiled as he admitted his initial efforts had focused on forward propulsion and steering control but failed to consider the need for braking. Oops!

Darryl's visionary genius was clearly on display when, as you have already heard, he created an oven for Mama. That incredible feat demonstrates Darryl's ability to consider a problem, visualize a solution, create a prototype, and continue to build and modify based on research, new information, and field conditions. If you do not believe that was truly an extraordinary accomplishment, stop for a moment and consider what occurred in that case: a *squirrel* created an oven by conducting research, overcoming obstacles (little things like the inability to access electricity, fire – any energy source that might typically power an oven), using existing rudimentary materials (a cracked glass bowl for a lens), and performing complex calculations regarding optimal positioning to harness the power of the sun to achieve temperatures equivalent to an oven you or I might use at home. A *squirrel* did that.

After further discussion and a series of similar stories, I had Darryl complete a battery of standard cognitive assessments. I started with a few basic instruments: the Stanford-binet, Woodcock-Johnson, Kaufman, Wechsler, and Differential Ability Scales, before moving on to Raven's Progressive Matrices and some complex mathematical modeling. Then I reviewed the data from these assessments individually and as a group using multivariate analysis of variance to test hypotheses on several variables. I was frankly stunned by the results! My professional opinion based on a very thorough and comprehensive analysis: Holy Shit! This squirrel is off the freakin' chart! When we moved on to some advanced math problems and extremely complex equations, Darryl was able to solve each one instantly, as though he had visualized the entire mathematical process. Now, I'm no dummy and no expert at math. Hell, I couldn't tell you how many avocados are in a guacamole! But I *do* know when objective, quantifiable data tells me I am in the presence of a very amazing and gifted individual…uh, I mean *animal*.

Spending time with others in the scurry, I heard numerous anecdotes about Darryl, and each one only served to reinforce how gifted he was. One that really stood out came from a conversation I had with Artemis and Mama. It began awkwardly, as Artemis was afraid anything he might say could land Darryl in trouble. I assured him that was not the case.

"Well, then…now, I ain't no snitch, but I'm tellin' ya Darryl might…I'm just saying *might*, you know – *allegedly* have knowledge about *fermentation*." That comment certainly piqued my interest! To provide some additional clarification and context, from the stories I heard in getting to know each of the squirrels, I learned that over time squirrels were able to create a fermented beverage concoction using a base of nut milk, similar to almond or soy milk. I had to learn more about it!

"What does that mean exactly, Artemis? What makes you say that?" I tried to keep my questions open-ended to elicit elaboration.

"Well, *you didn't get it from me*, but I was talkin' to some ole-timers who told me Darryl created some newfangled contraption and way to distill spirits."

"You mean he created a *still*? He built a still to create moonshine?"

"Moonshine, sunshine, nutshine – whatever you wanna call it. I'm just sayin' I heard he knew how to do all that…*allegedly*. I can't say for sure. I ain't no snitch."

"Do you know if his 'contraption' actually worked?"

"Oh, it worked alright! I mean, I *heard* it did. He makes a helluva dirty nut-tini! Uh…you know…I mean *allegedly*."

Mama nodded her approval. "Delicious! Best nut juice concoctions I've ever tasted…I mean *heard* about. That young squirrel didn't just fall off the turnip truck. He's sharp as a tack, bless his heart."

I didn't think it appropriate to ask Sam about the (alleged) nut juice apparatus, but I did have an opportunity to ask the adolescent female squirrel, Emma, about it. Interestingly, she seemed a little nervous, looking around and checking to make sure no one (no *squirrel*) was listening, before responding. "Maybe Darryl helped me out a few times with some beverages. I don't really know how he got them or made them, but the girls and the rest of the squirrels at the party… uh, I mean *picnic* really enjoyed them. I'm not sure what was in the juice, but I liked the way it made me feel. We all must have danced for hours!"

Hmmm…I wasn't quite sure I was ready to sample this (alleged) creative nut juice concoction, but I have to admit I was curious to find out if it was all it was cracked up to be.

Seventeen

Chad

When one's dead, one's dead... This squirrel
will become earth all in his time.
And still later on there'll grow new trees
from him, with new squirrels skipping about in
them. Do you think that's so very sad?

~ Tove Jansson

If Darryl is the genius of the group and at least according to Sam, Chad is most definitely at the other end of that spectrum. While the story Sam painted of Chad initially sounded like he may have come up short on the squirrel intelligence scale, I suspect a combination of hereditary and environmental factors might be at play. For example, I would note that a squirrel's brain is about the size of a walnut, and my not-so-precise scientific comparison to that of a human reminds me that for a squirrel, much of that processing capacity is focused on basic survival skills. Applying the "we only use 10% of our brain" hypothesis to a squirrel tells us there is not much left to work with from the start, which might further explain Chad's sad case. I knew there must be more to the story.

In fairness, Sam was quick to share one possible explanation for the fact that Chad is, in Sam's words "special". First, a little refresher and background from my earlier research. Eastern gray squirrels typically nest in tree hole cavities or nests built of leaves and twigs, high up in the top fork of a tree or fork of larger limbs. Male squirrels reach breeding age at just 9-11 months and females typically breed at between 6-8 months old. Squirrels generally mate twice a year from December to February and from May to June. Often, a mating "chase" is involved, with several males closely tracking a female as she moves throughout the day, in many ways similar to the human bar and dance club scene. Gray squirrels are polygamous, with males mating with several females, similar to some of the human... oops, sorry! The gestation period lasts approximately 40-45 days. In Florida, gray squirrel litters range in size from 2-6, and newborn squirrels are *altricial*, meaning they are born hairless and completely helpless. In some cases, squirrel moms may often move their litters back and forth between different den and nest locations in an effort to avoid predators, insects, or parasites, as well as any extreme changes in the weather. In the warm Florida climate, Florida gray squirrels have two litters per year and are not generally impacted by harsh winter conditions, as may occur with others farther north. The young squirrels are weaned within two months, and that brings us back to Chad.

Chad was born in a Spring litter with 3 other siblings and was noticeably smaller than the others. Chad's mom was widely known to frequent some less than reputable establishments, where the nut juice flowed freely and females drank for free, with contests and promotions designed specifically to lure in the more lucrative male suitors. Chad's mom was known to shake her bushy tail for just about anyone, and word on the street was that she had a fling with a chipmunk, which might explain Chad's small size, large cheek pouches, and slightly brownish fur. At every low-end squirrel bar, the well-known floozy spent her time downing free drinks, dancing and gyrating well after sundown to the rhythmic sounds of tree frogs and crickets. As a result, when she returned late at night, if at all, the four helpless young offspring often squirmed and jostled for a coveted nipple position. Squirrels typically feed their babies every 2-4 hours and in Chad's case, even if he got his turn at a teat, it was probably infrequent, not to mention the mother's milk was laced with the aforementioned nut juice. We must therefore assume it is highly likely Chad was born with fetal nut syndrome (FNS). To make matters even worse, as a very vulnerable, blind, hairless, helpless infant, Chad was constantly and forcefully pushed around by his larger siblings who, after all, found themselves in the same untenable situation. Unfortunately, as I found through my earlier research, Chad's nest address was up high in the crook of a large oak tree, at least 30-40 feet off the ground. (You can see where this is headed...)

One night during a typical Florida fall rainstorm, when Chad was about 5 weeks old and just after Chad's mom had returned home from a raucous night at some low-branch party, Chad muscled his way into the chow line and felt his way to the closest nipple available. Unfortunately, his much larger brother had precisely the same idea, and pushed Chad aside just as he was about to lock on, sending Chad tumbling uncontrollably to the back of the line. To make matters worse, the wet, tumbling youngster rolled right over the top of his sibling sister, who squealed, squeaked, and cried, which then caused the other members of the starving litter to buck and jerk.

At that point the scene was like a tube of toothpaste being squeezed sequentially, creating a slow but very powerful cascading wave of squirrel babies, with Chad in the worst possible position near the opening. Groping and grabbing at anything with his little undeveloped paw claws, Chad managed to scratch and thoroughly piss off a bigger, stronger sister, who absolutely was not having it! Her shrill shriek (say *that* a few times!), accompanied by a forceful rear leg thrust, sent Chad sliding toward the precipice. Grabbing at any leaf or twig his little legs and paws could manage, he was able to temporarily stabilize the squirrel avalanche, and the flow subsided...uh, well...until a tiny shred of an oak leaf found its way to a resting spot precisely at the tip of Chad's tiny nostrils. There it remained, buoyed by the continuing soft rain and warm Florida breeze, a perfectly positioned irritant that formed the trigger for a catastrophic involuntary response, an unavoidable innate reflex action designed to ensure the infant nose remains clear of any obstruction that might impact breathability. The inescapable laws of physics and determinism, the inevitability of action and reaction... yep, you just can't stop a sneeze!

At five weeks old, Chad's poor little eyes were just beginning to process light versus darkness, but as we all know, *they're surely about to slam shut during a sneeze.* For poor Chad, the lights went out as soon as the sneeze explosion occurred, as the small but compressed force caused Chad's small frame to be ejected backwards, like the recoil and ejection of a just-fired cartridge from a rifle. In a scene that no-doubt resembled a slow-motion burst from an exploding water balloon, Chad was forced back, bursting through the stick-and-leaf framework that held the nest together. Clearing the nest edge (feel free to insert "hanging Chad" jokes here), he soon found himself in complete freefall, the worst imaginable way for a young squirrel to experience the inexorable principle of gravity. One can only imagine how completely terrified and disoriented this poor fragile, innocent, undeveloped baby squirrel must have been as it hurtled toward the ground below.

Fortunately, whether the result of divine providence or the fact that oak trees lose their leaves in the fall, the shallow mound of leaves at the base of the tree served as a pillow to cushion the inevitable crash. Poor Chad must have bounced several times before coming to rest face down in the wet grass, a feeling I know all too well from my accident. If a poor defenseless little squirrel does not concern you, let me assure you that there are so many owls, hawks, buzzards, bobcats, coyotes, dogs, cats, numerous snake species, and all sorts of sadistic neighborhood kids that would love to get their hands on such an unfortunate and vulnerable creature. Summary: Chad was in deep shit!

Obviously, having only recently been introduced to Chad by Sam, I know the young squirrel survived, but the intense story Sam recounted was nothing short of miraculous. It seems that following Chad's untimely fall from grace, the next morning as he lay motionless on the grass, stunned and still in shock, the daughter of the neighbor immediately adjacent to the park was waiting for the school bus and saw several crows fly down to check out something on the ground in the park, just on the other side of the hedge separating the two properties. If, like me, you are pondering the odds of that young girl being at that exact spot at that exact time, I couldn't agree more. Fortunately, children are naturally curious, and it was that childish curiosity that alerted the young girl to investigate. As she approached the park, the birds quickly departed, and she observed the pitiful scene: a baby squirrel, still at least partially blind and mostly hairless, all alone, squinting in the morning sunlight and making noises best described as cries for help, with no way of knowing whether it was injured, abandoned, or both. The girl immediately screamed for her mother, who quickly arrived on the scene as they continued to assess the situation, wondering out loud: "What happened? Where is its mother?" They scanned the immediate vicinity and soon decided the only recourse was to bring a basket and soft towel to cradle the little squirrel until they could figure it all out.

After considerable mother-daughter discussion, bickering, and negotiation, it was agreed that no – the girl could *not* stay home from school to play nurse to a baby squirrel, that the mom would do everything she could to care for the fragile patient, with no promise or guarantee it would survive the day. There would be no veterinarian ambulance or ER – just the loving care of a family who cared deeply about all creatures, great and small. Yes, even *squirrels*. You can imagine the rest of the story – days, weeks, and months of care, feeding, cuddling, laughs, tears, and hopefulness, as the young squirrel responded to the love it was shown and slowly but surely demonstrated it had recovered fully and was ready to be reintroduced to "the wild" (as if that designation applied at all to a park in a suburban Florida neighborhood). Thanks to the kindness and support of these caring neighbors, Chad sniffed, scratched, and climbed his way up that familiar tree and was reunited with his siblings, but mom was nowhere to be found.

Now, to be perfectly clear, the poignant story of Chad's horrific and unfortunate accident cannot possibly fully explain, nor will we ever actually know, what impact it may have had on his early squirrelhood development and cognitive abilities. I can only present to you the information Sam shared with me, coupled with my personal observations. I cannot make any judgement or assumptions regarding the effect of Chad's mother's postnatal care or possible adverse lifestyle impact, other than Sam's report that the mom did eventually check herself into squirrel rehab and just passed the one-year sobriety mark as nut-juice free. Sam spoke with her recently and said he was confident she was no longer a nut case.

Chad's lack of social skills has apparently resulted in other squirrels teasing poor Chad as awkward and stupid, but I believe the issue is more his lack of a male role model and the training a young male squirrel would normally receive from his parents and others in the scurry. The fact his early upbringing was largely shaped by a well-intentioned young girl who frequently used Chad for dress-up sessions, constantly changing hair and tail styles and nail colors, and hanging out with Barbie may have triggered gender identity issues. But on a positive note, apparently he does know the words to every Taylor Swift song…

Unfortunately, while most squirrels are normally incredibly nimble and react quickly to danger, Chad's lack of early squirrel education and training, coupled with a possible cognitive processing deficit might potentially create a truly life-threatening situation, especially if he is asked to participate in any "roadway incursions" or other similar tasks that might require lighting fast reflexes. As is the case with humans, the interplay between "nature and nurture" for a squirrel like Chad means that whatever biological and genetic factors may be present must be supported with real world experience, with the sort of on-the-job squirrel training that comes from his exposure to environmental factors and learning from others in the scurry. Sam indicated he is always looking for ways to involve Chad more in team activities.

As I continued to have the opportunity to observe Chad's interaction with the scurry group, it was certainly something I would be watching closely.

Eighteen

Emma

You can't be friends with a squirrel! A squirrel is
just a rat with a cuter outfit.

~ Sarah Jessica Parker

As with Darryl's role as the intellectual savant of the
scurry, it seems there is also a slacker and clueless
member in almost every group. For our squirrel research
subjects, that characterization fits Emma perfectly.
Emma is a Gen Z adolescent female, a teenager in
squirrel years, who is quick to let any squirrel that will
listen know she identifies as nonbinary, and for whom
the practical world of squirrel development and survival
is simply an annoyance. In fact, I suspect if the squirrel
alphabet and dictionary extended beyond "z", Emma's
picture would likely be found there. Her mother
Samantha is put off by Emma's constant protestations
and argumentative tone when asked to do the most minor
tasks. But from listening to both Sam and Samantha, that
was not always the case. In fact, during my conversation
with Samantha, she was quick to point to Emma's active
participation when she was younger. I was surprised
when she said:

"Emma was always a good squirrel who had lots of friends and was involved in all sorts of activities. She sold *Squirrel Scout* cookies for her troop, participated in squirrel sports, and could have probably qualified for aerial gymnastics in the Squirrelympics, but in the last year or so, she seems more interested in boy squirrels, if you know what I mean."

Mama chimed in: "That girl is pretty as a pumpkin but half as smart. She's got the looks but not the brains, bless her heart."

Apparently several members of the scurry and some of Emma's friends encouraged her to go into modeling, and I was definitely starting to get the impression Emma must be regarded as highly attractive and desirable by other squirrels. Naturally, my brain tried to envision parallels to human interactions, though I was unable to imagine what an effective pick-up line might be for male squirrels: "Your paw looks heavy, can I hold it for you?" or maybe "Do you have a map? I just got lost in your eyes." I wonder how many approaches focus on "tail"? No, let's not go there.

From what Samantha described, I concluded that Emma was simply experiencing puberty which, at least in humans, is shaped by both social and biological factors. I suppose it is possible Emma's pubertal tempo may have resulted in her being an "early bloomer", which may also explain the hormonal swings her mother reported and help explain her remarkable descent from an admirable young female member of the scurry to a petulant, disrespectful teenager. Samantha related a recent incident where Emma was asked to help with the scurry's chores, specifically to help tidy up what would be the human equivalent of Baby's crib, a small sleeping area in the nest adjacent to Sam and Samantha. Her response was deemed unacceptable.

"OMG, not again! Like, like why can't someone else do it for a change? Why do I get stuck cleaning up Baby's mess at the time? This is, like so lame!"

To which Samantha immediately responded: "Oh, you poor thing! That task isn't in your imagined job description? Guess what? Putting up with your whiny bullshit isn't in mine."

"Samantha don't play!" Rambo snickered as he covered his mouth with his tail.

"Yeah, whatever!" Emma complained as she turned her back to show the others her erect tail, like a human might extend our center finger, and swung it from side to side as she retreated and scurried away, grudgingly accepting her assignment like a form of punishment.

Mama chimed in: "That girl can kiss my go-to-hell. Somebody surely needs to jerk a knot in her tail and tan her hide!" Samantha was embarrassed, and Mama sized up the situation.

"Hun, sometimes she hasn't got the sense God gave a goose. Don't let her get your goat. She will grow out of it, but in her case that might take a while, bless her heart."

Artemis was quick to offer his old-school advice: "I swear that young'n could make a preacher cuss! She's always actin' too big for her britches. I'm tellin' you, back in the day…" his voice trailed off as he lost his train of thought and wandered off.

In my observations and in noting her interactions with the other squirrels, Emma spent most days grooming her tail, complaining about running up and down trees wreaked havoc on her brightly painted pawnails, and occasionally trying to bum a nut snack from the others. This, of course, generally resulted in some terse exchanges and admonishments from the group, including what I can only assume were loud but unintelligible squirrel expletives. Samantha confirmed that Emma always sneaks away to hang out with her girlfriends who, according to Samantha, are not helping the situation. Apparently they call themselves the *Squirrel Girls,* a group of aspiring young would-be models who claim they are squirrel influencers for fashion, music, and just about anything else. It is the "anything else" that make Samantha and Mama nervous, and Emma has been known to push the envelope with her risqué and flirtatious behavior. Keep in mind the fact that male squirrels definitely do not need that type of additional stimulation.

Curious to understand more, in one case I was able to eavesdrop on Emma's conversation with a group of adolescent female squirrels, most likely the ones

Samantha was referring to. I was completely hidden by a poorly maintained hedge but had a perfect view, well within earshot of the group. Frankly, I felt like I needed some type of Gen Z squirrel translation utility app to truly understand the discussion. I heard:

"Hey sis, what you gonna do 'bout what Sophie cappin?"

"Girl don't know shit. She's weird af."

"Vibe check that bitch. She's sus."

Another chimed in: "You saw her glow up? She goin' after Mark?"

"Big yikes! She draggin' him, totally."

"Let's check out that new shop. I hear it's bussin."

"I got you, bestie! You bring the guap."

I did make a few notes, all the while thinking "Wait! What the hell was that?"

I suppose you might think of Emma and her *Squirrel Girl* friends as the species GenS, a generation of adolescent squirrels eager to experience all they can get away with and, of course, drive their parents nuts (sorry) in the process. As might occur in similar human challenges, I could see that Samantha and Mama have teamed up to provide the support, counseling, and direction to help guide Emma and steer her toward her more positive areas of interest, which include nutrition, tail styling, and using her gymnastic skills with Rambo's self-defense training.

Mama assured me she was committed to helping Emma achieve her goals and aspirations, provided she follows some basic rules and, in Mama's words:

> "Sometimes that girl can make a preacher cuss! She goes through boyfriends faster than a hot knife through butter. She needs to worry less about getting' all gussied up and more about helping with the chores around here, bless her heart."

From what I was able to observe, although Emma often rebels against authority like many adolescents, she has a great deal of respect for Mama and her no-nonsense advice.

One thing is for sure: for this troupe to succeed as a team, every squirrel will need to pull their weight, and Emma is no exception.

Nineteen

A Day in the Life (of a squirrel)

I love my squirrel and dumplings, but you
can make it with chicken and dumplings.
I love making the dumplings. I think I
just like to roll out dough.

~ Kay Robertson

As my conversation with Sam continued, I could sense that as we were getting to know each other, he and the others had now determined I was not a threat, creating an atmosphere of trust and mutual respect. Up until this point I had purposely avoided asking the obvious question: *"What the hell did you think were you doing when your middle of the road stunt almost killed me?"* But now I was starting to think this might the time to at least ease into the discussion. My goal, of course, was to stick to my original research mission in an effort to understand the squirrels' true motivation for such dangerous behavior, which clearly represents a threat to both the squirrels and unsuspecting human drivers (like me!).

Not wanting to create any direct confrontation, I started by asking Sam to describe a typical day in the life of the scurry, explaining I wanted to gain some additional insight into each squirrel's contribution to the group. Sam seemed to be expecting the question, appeared very relaxed, and responded almost immediately.

"Ah yes, your research. Sure, let's start with an overview, and then we can get into specifics and answer questions. Does that sound like a plan?"

Holy shit! How amazing is this? It's like I'm talking to a colleague or conducting an interview with a business owner or the chief executive of a major company or other organization…except I'm talking to a *squirrel*! Oh yeh, and *the squirrel is talking to me!*

"That sounds great! I'm guessing you guys get up pretty early." Wait, *what*? What the hell did I just say? I'm asking if *squirrels* wake up *early*? Seriously? Sam smiled, or maybe that was a smirk…hard to tell.

"Yes, I guess you could say that. As you might imagine, we hunker down at night – safety in numbers, and all. There are a lot of nocturnal predators out there, so we all stick close together and stay on high alert. You probably already know from your research that we rely on our sense of hearing, which has a range of about 2 ½ times that of you humans."

I pause here to share an interesting quirk I observed on several occasions during the course of conversations with both Sam and several other members of the group. Whenever Sam or the other squirrels said the word "human", they pronounced it *"hooman"* (as in *"who"*). I have no idea why that is or why I mention it here now, but it struck me as odd. As I pondered the phenomenon, Sam continued his overview.

"If any squirrel in the scurry hears even the slightest sound, they sound an initial alert, at a level just audible enough for the rest of the group. Sometimes that makes for a restless night, especially when the owls are around." Wow, I hadn't thought of that!

"The other major nighttime threat are the damn bobcats. We hate those monsters! They're like feline ninjas, I'm tellin' you!" As Sam continued, I found myself feeling pretty uninformed, ignorant, clueless, and insensitive, having thought little about the dangers these animals face every night.

"But to answer your question, Doc, when the sun comes up, we're all headed out, except for Samantha, who stays in the nest to take care of Baby."

As Baby heard his name, I heard a chirping noise coming from his direction, something like a dog's squeaky-toy might make. I saw Samantha smile, then turn away with Baby actively nursing and accompanied by all sorts of loud slurping noises, punctuated by an occasional burp.

"For most of the morning, all of us are focused on gathering food, which we all share."

That prompted me to follow up with the obvious question: I wondered what's on the menu.

"From my research, I know squirrels are omnivores. Can you tell me about the types of food you typically find in this area?"

Sam shared that most of their diet consisted of nuts, seeds, and fruits, but he emphasized that squirrels also eat various insects, caterpillars, eggs, and even small animals and snakes. Yummy!

Sam explained that the scurry was most active during early morning and evening before dark. Depending on the season and especially during the summer, mid-day was a time of rest, and Sam shared that the scurry often planned group events for mid-morning or mid-afternoon get-togethers. That made my ears perk up, and I took the opportunity to probe further.

"So, I would love to hear more about the social events you plan as a group. What kinds of things do you typically do together?" Sam moved over beside me, out of earshot from the others, which is really saying something for a group of squirrels.

"Well, I guess you might say our activities fall into several categories. From what we have observed about humans, many of our get-togethers are actually quite similar to yours. We might plan what you call a picnic, and each of us brings something to share with the group. For example, Samantha and I usually mix up some nut butter (our secret recipe), and of course we bring some sweet treats for Baby. Darryl always seems to have the latest intel on where the ripe berries are, and Chad makes sure we have water and nut juice. Rambo always surprises us with some tasty insects; I'm really not sure how he captures them. Emma…well, Emma says she's in charge of 'tunes', which means she'll pick a radio station nobody else likes."

"Wait, radio? You guys have a radio?" I was puzzled, and I'm sure it showed.

"Sure. Rambo scored some old wristband player thing a human woman must have dropped while she was jogging around the neighborhood, at least that's what he *told* us. If you ask me, I bet the truth is he grabbed it out of her purse when some girls were playing on the pickleball court over there." Sam motioned with his paw toward the court next to our community pond and fountain. "He came back with the Bluetooth headphones and everything. Of course, for us those work just fine – no big speakers necessary."

"Wow, it sounds like you guys really know how to plan a party."

Sam nodded in agreement. "It just seems to work. Everyone knows their place and what to do."

I nodded and volunteered: "Sounds like fun, and yes – we do the same kinds of things with our friends."

Sam smiled broadly, his incisors glistening in the sunlight.

"Yes, and we love it when you do them here in the park. We always find plenty to eat when you leave!" We both shared a chuckle.

"Sam, what other types of things does the scurry do as a group?" I tried to ask the question in an open-ended way, with a goal of hearing about anything that might involve street activities, but not suggesting anything in particular.

"Well, at the risk of living up to what you may consider a stereotype, we do love activities that involve a challenge." Aha! Here we go!

"Really, like what?" I leaned closer, listening intently.

"Our favorite is the bird feeder challenge course. As a team building exercise, I especially like it because it really has everyone on the same level, sort of like you humans with your bowling." (No, I didn't ask how he knew that.) Sam explained further:

"We usually compare notes on the status of various feeders at nearby homes and discuss which ones represent the best opportunity for success. Then I'll ask Darryl to check out a few. He's really good with the technical details, and we will get together to review everything. You know, like how high is the pole? Is it close to any tree limbs for an aerial approach? Do they have a cat? What times are the owners usually not at home? Are there cameras? We talk through several possible options, but then it's pretty much every squirrel for themselves. Each gets just one shot at the feeder. If any attempt is interrupted by a human, domestic pet, or other unforeseen problem, we retreat and regroup, always watching each other's back."

"Wow, I had no idea!"

"Over the years it's become so popular, we even created a league and compete with other squirrel scurries throughout the neighborhood. So far this year we are in second place. That clan on the other side of the pond recruited a couple of young squirrel pros from the next town over. Word is they have mad scamper skills!"

"Well, I'll have to get tickets for that competition!" I laughed at the thought of attending such a *squirrelympics*, trying to picture squirrels receiving a gold medal, probably in the shape of an acorn.

"When it gets cooler, I plan to do some recruiting up north. If we can get a decent draft pick for at least one *flying squirrel* this year, that could be a real game changer! Drop in from above! Can you imagine?" Sam's eyes were wide with excitement as he spread his arms wide mimicking a glider, before realizing how silly that looked.

"Hey, you know what? We're doing a new team bird feeder briefing later this morning. Wanna come?"

"A bird feeder? Some kind of training?"

"Yes, you'll see. I hope you will join us. I think you will find it interesting. We'll meet at 11 on the other side of the park." Sam motioned with his paw, pointing in the general direction.

"Sounds like fun. I'll see you there."

I used the break in the interim to jot down some additional notes and put together a short list of questions I hoped would eventually lead to a discussion on the real focus of my research. I wanted to remain careful not to be too direct and confrontational, but now that I had established a good rapport and at least a sense of trust, I really wanted to begin to steer the conversation toward learning what motivates the squirrels to such risky roadway behavior. Maybe I will learn more at this bird feeder briefing.

Twenty

The Bird Feeder

Always be yourself… unless you can be a squirrel.
Then, be a squirrel.

~ Anonymous

Bird feeder raid orientation was scheduled for 11AM. Sam had given me directions to the meeting area on the opposite side of the community park, and I must have spent the better part of an hour trying in vain to get my phone working before going to catch up with the group. Something weird was definitely going on, because I still had no cell coverage – zero bars, which meant no communication, but at least I could get some pictures and video with my iPhone. I grabbed my notepad from my bag and arrived at a small clearing, well away from the paved walkway. The scurry was there when I arrived, and Sam was positioned on what appeared to be the remnants of an old fencepost, checking the roster and making sure all squirrels were present. He nodded to acknowledge my presence, then addressed the group to explain the morning's exercise.

"Today we will be following up on a new location Darryl has been scouting over the past week. Come on up Darryl and tell us what you found."

Darryl came forward, and I noticed he was carrying a long straight stick and holding a round piece of plastic. On closer inspection, I could see what looked like a jar lid or some type of plastic cover with a hole in the center. Hmmm…that's odd. I wondered what that was about.

"Thank you, Sam. I have to tell you I am pretty excited about this one. You know the green house on the cul-de-sac, the one with the white picket fence?"
I watched as Sam, Samantha (holding Baby), Mama, Emma, Chad, and Rambo all nodded affirmatively.
Rambo said: "The one with that Siamese cat?"
As Rambo said the word "cat", Baby let out a shriek and squirmed in Samantha's arms, almost knocking her over. Regaining her balance, I could hear her softly scolding and rocking Baby, who continued squirming as Samantha held him more firmly and rocked him gently in her arms.
Rambo snarled: "I hate that damn cat!"
"Yes, that's the one." Darryl continued. "The cat almost always sits on the back of the living room sofa facing the front window. The feeder is in the back, so that should not be an issue."
Sam asked: "Do we know if anyone will be home?"
"Great question!" Darryl flashed a toothy grin as he continued. "I have watched the house every day for the past week. Apparently, the owner is taking flying lessons, and she has scheduled training Monday, Wednesday, and Friday from 10AM until Noon. She

leaves the house at 9:30 and usually isn't back until after about 1:30, sometimes later."

Samantha asked: "That's incredible! How did you learn all that?" Frankly, I shared her amazement and wondered the same thing.

Darryl was beaming. "Thanks. It's just observation, really. On the days she has training, she feeds the cat just before she leaves. I know that because that's when the cat leaves his perch in front of the window, and he returns to the back of the sofa at around 9:40. If we plan to hit the feeder at 10AM, we should not have any problems."

Sam was impressed. "That's great info, Darryl. Tell us, how in the world did you find out she was training at a flight school?"

Darryl held his head a bit higher and puffed his chest majestically. "That was easy. She drives a Lexus convertible and always has the top down. I was on a pine branch right next to the garage and could see everything clearly. Her iPhone calendar is always visible, and she puts her flight bag in the passenger seat. It's a big pink logoed duffle bag and clearly says *'Blue Sky Pilates'*."

As he divulged his methodology, Darryl had a huge grin on his face, proudly letting the others know he was obviously a master of the *Squirrelock Holmes* art of deduction. I didn't have the heart to tell him about the whole "pilot thing" and burst his bubble, and at least the schedule made sense, so I muffled my laughter with a cough and kept my mouth shut.

Sam began a round of applause and placed his paw on Darryl's shoulder, as a proud father might with his son. The scurry joined in the ovation, which was also notably punctuated with a loud fart coming from Baby's direction, causing the group to erupt in laughter.

Now, I pause here to note several points, just in case you were wondering:

1. At least in Darryl's case, squirrels are *extremely* observant.
2. How the hell can they tell *time*? What's up with that?
3. Maybe they are not quite as smart as I thought. *They obviously can't spell.*

As I was pondering these astute observations, things got progressively weirder, if that is even possible.

Darryl moved over to a sandy area near a fence boundary, with the group gathering around. Using the long stick he was carrying, he began scratching in the sand, and I soon realized he was drawing a diagram! OMG! This guy was like a general addressing the troops and sketching out a battle plan! He quickly outlined the footprint of the house relative to the driveway and street. Then, like a freakin' football coach diagraming plays, he drew an X in the back yard to show the feeder location. As he did so, he then took the round plastic piece he had been carrying and attached it to the end of the stick, before pushing the other end into the soft sandy soil. I noticed the plastic lid was the top of a mayonnaise jar, now inverted on the end of the stick like a shallow bowl.

Darryl placed a few tiny rocks in the lid, announcing "This is the feeder. In this case it's a *Wild Birds Unlimited EcoTough Classic* hopper feeder, with a 2.5 quart capacity. The good news, my friends, is that this pilot lady buys only premium bird seed!"

Again, the scurry erupted with all sorts of clicks, squeaks, and tail gestures voicing their approval.

"Yes, that means sunflower seeds, safflower and *peanuts*!" Trust me, as soon as they heard the word "peanuts", it was pandemonium! Hell, he had me at *sunflower seeds*.

As Darryl continued to share the details of the bird feeder target, I glanced around the group and found each squirrel was listening attentively to every word, except Emma, who was focused on polishing her pawnails and filing them to even sharper points. Of course, that could be useful for extreme climbing, but her obvious lack of interest in the mission at hand told me that was not exactly what she had in mind.

"Oh, I almost forgot to mention, the feeder pole has a *baffle*." There was an immediate audible gasp. Now, in case you may not be familiar with bird feeders, as a way to prevent squirrels from climbing up the feeder pole, a baffle is a large inverted bowl-shaped dome, like a cake cover, made of plastic or metal that is fastened to the bowl below the feeder. A squirrel can climb the pole, but the baffle makes it impossible to get around it to continue up the pole. There are any number of baffle designs and other similar deterrents (such as greasing the feeder pole), each with a goal of preventing squirrels from being able to reach the feeder. So Darryl had clearly shocked the group by announcing that this extremely critical and seemingly insurmountable obstacle was part of today's mission. Samantha was the first to voice concern: "A baffle! How in the world are we supposed to get around a baffle?"

"Have a little faith, please." Darryl smiled as he turned to face the group and he panned slowly across to ensure he had every squirrel's complete attention. He stopped and scowled when he got to Emma.

"Emma, are you with us?" He was visibly agitated. Emma was caught off guard, almost dropping her nail file. "Uh, yeh, sure. Like, whatever."

"How would you propose that we get around the baffle, Emma? Please tell us." Darryl was pissed! It reminded me of a teacher catching a student in the back of the class napping and calling them out in front of the entire class. The scurry turned their attention to Emma; all eyes were on her as she temporarily halted the nail project to respond. You could hear a pin drop.

"What? Me? Uh, I guess I would like…Um, I'm like…*baffled*!"

Now, I don't know about you, but I absolutely hate a smart-ass, except in cases when they have a snappy comeback. Even *I* had to admit that was a good one, and the group seemed to agree, except Darryl, who was clearly not amused.

"Perfect, then I guess we'll let you go up the pole first, and we'll watch as you figure it out."

"I was just, like kidding. How *do* you get around a baffle?"

"You don't!" Darryl snarled. Artemis, Chad, and Sam nodded, and Rambo smiled and shook his head, most likely from prior experience, I suppose. Samantha and Mama looked at each other with concern, sensing the rising tension in the group. Then Artemis joined the discussion.

"Ain't no gettin' 'round a damn baffle, don't waste your time. Back in the day, I been up and down 'bout every type of pole there is. Once they started puttin' the damn baffle on there, just ain't no way around it, period. Hell, I threw my back out one day tryin' to get around one of those fool things. Put me out of commission for a week!" Artemis continued a mumbling tirade as he sat back down, having gotten pretty worked up about it.

"Poor thing. He means well, bless his heart." Mama held her paw to her chest. I'm not exactly sure where a squirrel's heart is, but Mama was suggesting

Artemis had his in the right place. She continued "Poor thing, he's got his knickers all in a knot."

Samantha joined in "Emma sure didn't help." To which Mama nodded affirmatively before replying "That girl is pretty as a peach but surely not the sharpest tool in the shed, bless her heart."

After some additional banter and bickering, complaining about the baffle as an unsolvable problem, Sam had heard enough.

"OK, that's enough! We all know the problem with baffles. Something tells me Darryl wouldn't have brought it up unless he has an answer. *Do* you have an answer?" He looked straight at Darryl – a stern but hopeful gaze.

"Of course!" Darryl again scanned the faces, and this time even Emma was paying attention.

"As I was about to say before you all freaked out, I have an idea that might sound a little crazy, but if we can pull it off, it will allow us to make our approach from above, rather than trying to get around the baffle." I suddenly had a vision of a scene from *Mission Impossible*, with *Tom Cruise* dangling on a cable from the ceiling, mere inches from the floor.

Darryl looked around and saw every squirrel hanging on each and every word. You could almost feel the anticipation. He then scampered over to a dried-up bush, snapped off a branch, and stepped back to his sand diagram.

"You see, the pilot lady has two young children, a boy and a girl." The pilot reference still made me laugh and I wasn't sure where he was headed with this, but we were about to find out. The bewildered looks from the rest of the scurry told me they were wondering the same thing.

"Of course, the kids are in school during the day, so they won't be around." Nods from the group. "But when the kids are home, they enjoy playing in the backyard. Their mother likes to keep a watchful eye on them from the window, just like Samantha and Mama would do."

Samantha smiled and nodded, Baby let out a loud burp, and Mama immediately offered support for the human mother: "Oh, bless her heart."

Using the stick to continue his sand diagram, Darryl noted "And she also likes to watch birds on the feeder, which is why the swing set is here and a trampoline is here." Darryl drew two circles in the sand next to the stick feeder. I remember immediately thinking "Oh, shit! This ought to be good!"

"It is a little complicated, but we can use both to our advantage. I have taken the liberty of looking at several possible scenarios, and one looks pretty promising…or at least *possible*."

Over the next several minutes, Darryl walked us through a scenario that seemed so far-fetched, it sounded like it came from a scene in that same *Mission Impossible* movie, but with an extremely gifted squirrel filling in for Tom Cruise. Frankly, as Darryl walked the group through the plan, I am pretty sure my mouth was embarrassingly wide open in disbelief the entire time. As Darryl spoke, I was creating a visual image of how this complex operation would have to play out if it was to have any chance of success. Of course, as the only *human* present for the sandlot diagram play-calling, my perspective was completely different, and for reasons other than my obvious elevated point of view. This is how Darryl explained the intricate details:

"The trampoline is the key, but it is not positioned as close as I would like. However, after estimating its weight, even with all of us pushing at the same time, we simply wouldn't be able to move it." At that point I'm thinkin' "Kudos to you, Darryl and sorry, but I'm not about to volunteer." Fortunately, he never looked in my direction, and at that point I could see the group shared my desire to hear a better alternative.

"To make this work, we need to start with the swing set. According to my calculations, the swing can allow us to reach the trampoline, and we can then use it to bounce up to land on top of the feeder, which fortunately has a much larger footprint than my rudimentary prototype." He motioned with an outstretched paw to the inverted mayonnaise lid, which promptly fell off the stick, sending the small rocks scattering about. That elicited some nervous laughter from the group, which surprisingly did not seem at all phased by the presentation. Darryl went on to explain in considerable detail how a squirrel could potentially be launched from the swing set, use the trampoline, and so on. With your permission and apologies for what might seem like *mansplaining*, I hope you will view it more like *humansplaining*, or rather simply my interpretation of what I heard and observed.

Bear with me and, especially if you are a visual person, try to envision the following mental image, in a slow-motion movie, step-by-step:

1. A squirrel is selected to be the point squirrel for the assault on the feeder.
2. That squirrel is equipped with two important pieces of equipment: a coiled length of lightweight ¼ inch rope, and a homemade backpack with a special rudimentary parachute, fashioned from an old handkerchief and some string.
3. The lead squirrel takes his or her place on the swing.
4. The other squirrels form two groups, which will pull the swing back initially, then alternate in pushing and pulling, in order to create the most extreme swing height and arc possible.
5. While on an upward trajectory and at the absolute zenith, the lead squirrel releases from the swing at precisely the right time, capitalizing

on the upward momentum and achieving maximum height as he or she is catapulted toward the trampoline. Other than outstretched arms and legs for minor in-flight adjustments, the trajectory to the trampoline landing zone must be precise.

6. On the final approach to the trampoline, the lead squirrel pulls in his/her arms and legs, forming a squirrel cannonball, thus creating maximum density and minimizing atmospheric resistance.

7. On contact with the trampoline, the squirrel remains in the balled-up position and remains so until he or she first senses the initial upward bounce. At that point the rear legs thrust outward and downward, creating additional thrust and acceleration.

8. After reaching the apogee, the squirrel deploys the handkerchief parachute, using the control strings to maneuver to the feeder target.

9. Using all four paws to securely grasp the feeder, the squirrel the secures one end of the rope and lowers the other end to the ground.

10. At least one squirrel climbs the rope to assist the lead. Together they push the seed mixture over the edge of the feeder, and all members of the group gather and retreat with the loot, along with the two rappelling down from the feeder, avoiding any contact with cats or other animals,

competing squirrels, and local law enforcement or neighborhood security patrols.

Now, as you are no doubt thinking I have just described an amazing act from *Squirrel du Soleil*, consider that, at least to me as an observer, what I found more amazing was the fact that the squirrels did not seem in any way bothered by the detailed description Darryl outlined. In fact, after the presentation and discussion, while I was thinking "What the f—k?", the squirrels were calmly asking specific questions.

Rambo wanted to know the precise distance between the trampoline and "the target".

Samantha asked about the weather forecast, as clouds had formed since the discussion began.

Chad was curious how the lead squirrel would be selected.

Mama wanted to know how the group could possibly carry all of the seed back to the park and up in the tree. She did, however, assure everyone she had a great recipe for birdseed pie.

Artemis wanted us all to know he had pulled off an identical plan "back in the day", well..except for the swing, trampoline, and parachute part.

Emma asked if she could hang out on the trampoline for a while afterwards and said she would catch up with everyone later.

Baby…well, Baby was agitated, bucking and squirming around uncontrollably, so Samantha took him behind the bushes for a pee.

After the Q&A session wrapped up, Sam stepped to the front and said:

"Great job, Darryl! OK, everyone, are we ready to do this?" I thought "Oh my god! They are actually going to attempt this wacky plan!" Sam continued:

"The one thing we haven't discussed is who will run point on this operation. I have given it a lot of thought. We need a courageous volunteer who can become a squirrel cannonball, balled up so tight that when they fly high off the swing and hit the trampoline, the density will generate enough force on impact to create maximum bounce."

At that point I noticed Darryl was nodding in agreement, and the others were looking at each other, wondering which of them might be qualified for such a high honor, as Sam made his way past each squirrel, like a general inspecting the troops.

"It can't be someone too large (Rambo shook his head), too old (all eyes on Artemis), or too concerned about breaking a pawnail (double-take from Emma and loud group gaffaws). We need a courageous, fearless, compact squirrel, and I am proud to announce Chad has graciously volunteered for this auspicious assignment."

I watched as surprised looks appeared across the entire group, as Darryl started the slow applause, which soon increased in tempo as everyone including me joined in, applauding and cheering loudly. That included Chad, who joined in the celebration, seemingly temporarily oblivious to the ramifications of the announcement…until suddenly it hit him! There he was, poor thing, in mid-clap, trying to process what was happening. Sam walked over the shake paws, at which time Chad's dazed look morphed into a weird combination of shock, bewilderment, paralysis, and abject terror, as the realization hit him like a ton of bricks.

"Thank you, Chad for volunteering, and I know I speak for the entire scurry when I say how much we admire your bravery and appreciate you taking on this important assignment.

Sam continued speaking, as I focused on Chad and watched it all sink in. Chad opened his mouth to speak, but nothing came out for what seemed like an eternity, followed by a barely coherent stammering.

"I… uh, I…" Chad cocked his head as though he was trying to remember if he might have somehow forgotten a commitment he might have made. You know, like when you wake up with a terrible hangover, and later your friends tell you all the things you did at that wild party last night.

"Um… I *volunteered*? You picked *me*?"

Sam smiled and nodded. "Absolutely! You are perfect for this mission. Small, compact, experienced at dropping from high above…I can't imagine a better choice. Thank you for volunteering." The laughter from the group soon turned to applause and cheers, as Chad looked on, still completely bewildered as each squirrel approached him to offer congratulations, high-fours, and squirrel knuckle-bumps.

Mama shook her head and offered: "Poor thing. He couldn't find his ass with both paws in his back pockets, bless his heart."

As things settled down, Sam barked out a few assignments – Darryl would get the rope, Rambo would fashion the backpack and handkerchief parachute. Mama, Samantha, and Emma would fashion makeshift sacks from whatever fabric material they could recover from nearby trash bins. Sam instructed everyone to be ready to go at 9:30AM the following morning.

Oh, I *definitely* have to see this!

Twenty-one

It's show time!

People look at me like I'm a little strange,
when I go around talking to squirrels and
rabbits and stuff. That's ok. That's just ok.

~ Bob Ross

It seemed like morning appeared from out of nowhere.
Funny, I did not remember sleeping at all, which I
chalked up as excited anticipation to be able to witness
the bird feeder caper first-hand, like getting a last-minute
ticket to the big game. I wouldn't miss this for the world!
I arrived at the same meeting spot as the day before, and
it looked like I was the last to arrive. No, as I counted
heads, Emma had not arrived. Hmmm…she had seemed
genuinely interested at the mission planning session. Just
as that thought was fading, I saw her arriving through an
opening in the border edge, sporting something that
looked like a tie-dyed t-shirt, unusual, since squirrels
don't generally wear clothes. She joined Rambo, who
was completely decked out in full camouflage and
tactical vest, holding what I assumed was the backpack
handkerchief parachute. Darryl was nearby, and I could
see what looked like a length of clothesline-type rope

cord. Chad was standing between Samantha and Mama and looked pretty nervous. Hell, *I know I would be!* Based on what I saw at the planning session run-through, the whole thing seemed a lot like the guy who gets shot out of a cannon at the circus.

Sam briefly checked to make sure everything was in place, then simply said: "OK, let's do this."
I followed as the rest of the group headed off toward the target home location. Now, if you have not already created a visual image of this procession, please let me help. We have a group of eight adult squirrels and one baby, walking along single file on all fours from a community park through backyards in a gated community with an adult male human following close behind, like a caboose at the end of a train or the last float in a parade. In summary, a very odd spectacle, to say the least. As we approached the home of "the pilot lady" and right on cue, we saw the Lexus convertible pulling out of the driveway, disappearing around the corner toward the neighborhood exit. As the squirrels moved toward the backyard, I walked up the driveway toward the street to surreptitiously sneak a quick peek at the home's front window. There, on the back of a sofa facing into the room in front of the main window was – you guessed it – the cat. Shielded from view by a tall hedgerow, I crept toward the backyard, where the squirrels were already busy at work. Surveying the scene, it was precisely as Darryl had described. To the right, a swing set with two

swings and a sliding board, facing toward the center of the yard, with a trampoline in the center. Just past the trampoline, a steel pole with a large, fancy bird feeder, and…oh yes, a baffle on the pole about a foot beneath the bottom of the feeder. Several yards to the left of the feeder pole, a seating area with Adirondack chairs surrounded a fire pit, not the kind of setup that gets much use during a typical short, mild Florida winter. I stayed in the shadow of the house, watching as the mission preparation continued.

Darryl was standing upright in front of Chad, who was being helped into his backpack by Rambo, straightening the straps and cinching the wide belt across the front of Chad's waist, if that term even applies to a squirrel's belly. Darryl used what looked like a large safety pin as a carabiner onto which he hooked the coiled rope. Rambo pulled out a helmet fashioned from a walnut shell and secured it to Chad's head with some type of tape material. Chad looked like a weird mashup of a Boy Scout ready for a camping trip and a Mario Brothers video game character, not exactly a highly trained special ops squirrel soldier preparing to launch an all-out strategic assault. But as they say: it is what it is. Sam walked over to the much smaller Chad and placed his paws on Chad's shoulders and looked him straight in the eye. From my vantage point I could not hear what was said, but I was sure it must have been some sage wisdom words of encouragement and support.

Darryl escorted Chad over the swing set, where Samantha, Emma and Mama had taken up positions on either side of the swing that faced directly in line with the trampoline, with Baby sitting in the grass nearby, gumming what looked like a nut cookie and making weird purring noises. Sam and Rambo joined them, and Artemis claimed a shady spot on a nearby planter, where he loudly let everyone know:

"I swear, back in the day I'd be up that pole in a heartbeat. Weren't no baffles back then!"

As Chad got comfortable on the swing, he reached up and grasped both supporting chains with his paws, like he was holding on for dear life, all while the swing remained completely motionless. Rambo gave Chad a final once-over, checking the backpack straps, parachute release cord, and coiled rope, before offering a hearty slap on both shoulders to let him know he had passed inspection and was ready to go. Darryl retreated to a position at the base of the trampoline so that he could have an unobstructed view of the entire operation. As he gave a thumbs up (if squirrels *have* thumbs), Sam and Rambo each grabbed one side of the swing, pulling it backwards in the opposite direction from the trampoline. The initial motion startled Chad, who then gripped the chains even tighter as they then released the swing, propelling it forward where Mama, Samantha, and Emma reached up and sent the swing back in the opposite direction. As this slow rocking back and forth continued, the frequency increased, and the arc of the swing moved higher each time, eventually approaching the same level as the top of the swing set bar.

With things in full swing (sorry…couldn't resist), Darryl yelled out the command:

"Chad, get ready! Prepare to go on the next one. OK, ready… GO!"

Nothing. Chad was frozen, his paws gripping the chains so tightly, it looked like he was having a seizure, but the terrified look on his face confirmed he was simply scared shitless. The swing started its backwards ark, with Darryl screaming loudly as he scamped quickly toward the swing, carrying the same long stick he had used the day before to create the feeder pole mockup.

"OK, Chad. You HAVE to go on the next one, understand? You can do this!"

The swing reached the end of its backwards movement, and Sam and Rambo gave it what they hoped would be a final strong push forward. Just as Chad was accelerating toward the required release point, Darryl maneuvered directly below Chad, tracking his forward movement and thrusting the pointed tip of the stick upward as hard as he could. The perfectly aimed pointed projectile found its mark in Chad's left butt cheek (if squirrels *have* butt cheeks), which began a rather bizarre chain reaction.

First, was a loud cry, as one might expect when one's butt cheek has been punctured by a sharp object. Reflexively reaching for the point and pain of the penetration, Chad released his grip and brought both arms down concurrently, which caused his compact torso to be catapulted upward and forward, continuing in an upward trajectory on his way to the apex.

Darryl quickly scampered, running back toward the trampoline, yelling as he ran: "Chad, ball up! Ball up, buddy!" I really couldn't tell if the movement I saw as Chad flew like a missile overhead was actually him curling up in a ball as instructed or simply scrunching up his little body and covering his eyes out of abject fear. In either case I'd probably score him a solid eight for executing a decent tucked position. He held that pose on the downward trajectory as he reached terminal velocity and slammed into the center of the trampoline.

I heard Darryl yell "YES!" as we all watched the trampoline absorb the impact and stretch downward, before springing back up and flinging Chad high in the air, with his little arms and legs flailing around like crazy. Traveling rapidly upward, Chad could hear Darryl screaming at the top of his lungs: "Release the chute! Pop the chute!"

Immediately the others joined in: "Release the chute! Release the chute. Chad! Pull the cord! Pull it now!"

Not quite understanding the instructions, Artemis nevertheless quickly joined the chorus: "Shoot! Shoot! Pull the trigger!"

Now, I can't say for sure, but whether the result of pure adrenalin and self-preservation or some uncanny innate squirrel instinct, Chad pulled the cord! Oh my God, he pulled the cord!

Amazingly, the handkerchief parachute deployed precisely as designed, and I watched with my mouth wide open in disbelief as this small squirrel floated slowly, slowly in the direction of the bird feeder. Unbelievable!

At this point, the rest of the group had moved from the swing set to the area around the feeder pole, and all eyes were now on Chad's descent trajectory, which seemed pretty good but not quite 100% in line with the target. If you have ever watched a professional skydiver skillfully maneuver his parachute to land precisely on target, you've seen they use "toggles", handles they can pull to steer the chute. Well, Chad's handkerchief is doing great so far, but it did not come with a steering wheel, so it depends exclusively on the current wind direction and whatever body motion Chad is able to muster. That is especially unfortunate, since the look of terror on Chad's face has remained unchanged since the original swing launch. Darryl was frantic, barking commands for Chad to lean to the left or right, but Chad appeared catatonic and unresponsive., probably still in shock. As luck would have it, however, it appeared that due to the large size of the feeder the ample roof might just be a big enough target to facilitate a landing. Darryl continued shouting and as Chad suddenly became aware of his surroundings and current position relative to the feeder, he began frantically kicking his legs, which did absolutely, positively *nothing*. In spite of that, the light wind was moving the parachute in at least the general direction of the feeder roof. Seeing that, Darryl's yelling was more encouraging and supportive, but nonspecific, with phrases like "You got this! Almost there! Hang on! Get ready!", all with no real direction or context. Chad's response consisted of waving his arms and an odd running or pedaling motion with his hind legs. I am not sure if any change in direction actually occurred as a result, but we could all see it was going to be close.

Darryl was now trying to use his own body language as though to somehow affect control, like a bowler might do in trying to pick up a spare. Lower, lower… Chad was now just a few feet above the feeder. Slowly, down, down. Chad's little legs made contact with the roof of the feeder, but the homemade parachute was still pulling Chad, who was now sliding across the feeder roof, trying to use his hind paws to slam on the brakes. That was only partially successful, and the slide continued, moving perilously close to the roof edge. Leaning forward, Chad reached down and used his front claws in an attempt to grab hold, resulting in a sound best described as fingernails across a chalkboard. Clawing and scratching as best he could, dragging all fours, the reluctant paratrooper came to rest mere inches from the edge of the feeder roof. I felt like I was watching a scene from Mission Control. Ladies and gentlemen: *the squirrel has landed!* Can you imagine how cool it would have been if Chad would have had the composure to address the group cheering below? Just think!

In my head I was thinking *"That's one small step for squirrel, one giant leap for squirrelkind."* Unfortunately, not only was that *not* happening, once Chad was able to stand upright, he immediately threw up, and I'm pretty sure he crapped his… well, I think he shit himself. But, as they say, the crowd went wild, and the scurry broke into loud and sustained applause and cheering. And yes, in case you're wondering, I most definitely joined in. I was quite certain I was witnessing history.

I heard Mama exclaim: "Well, butter my butt and call me a biscuit!"
Artemis would not be outdone: "That's my boy! Taught him everything he knows!"

Once Chad regained his composure and was able to acknowledge the praise from his supporters, he climbed down from the feeder roof to the perch ledge where huge piles of seed flowed out from the feeder's center holding bin. He took the rope hanging from his pack, tied it off to one of the bird perch dowels, and dropped it down to the ground. Sam nodded to Rambo, whose muscles were in full display as he pulled himself up the rope, easily circumventing the infamous baffle, rendered completely ineffective as the rope hung well outside its nearby circumference. Simply incredible!

Once Rambo joined Chad on the main platform, he embraced Chad with a big squirrel hug, stopping just before little Chad's eyeballs seemed ready to pop out. Congratulations accomplished, the fun began in earnest. Sam yelled out "Let it rain, you guys!", and rain it did! What seemed like a never-ending avalanche of all sorts of seeds, grains and nuts were guided over the edge in waves, as Chad and Rambo were clearly enjoying being able to push huge piles to rain down on the group below, who immediately began gathering the treasure in the makeshift sacks until they were filled to capacity. It seemed like such a huge amount to carry, at least until Chad and Rambo rappelled down the rope to rejoin the group. Chad filled the backpack, while Rambo used the parachute handkerchief to create a huge bag, filling it completely, something only he could carry. Sam was quick to remind everyone that the mission was not complete until the getaway was successful, and the same single file procession returned from whence it came, but this time weighed down with the precious edible loot.

Then, in broad daylight, this scurry of squirrel bandits marched home having accomplished what surely had to have been one of the largest feeder heists of all time, to be forever etched in the annals of squirrel history. Back at the park, I watched as Sam congratulated each team member individually before offering some final words to the group.

"Today we showed that with proper preparation and teamwork, there is nothing we can't accomplish. Each of you should be proud of your role in making it happen, and I am so very proud of you all."

The group erupted in applause, chattering, and some really wacky tail waving. What might have become an all-night celebration was tempered with the fact that the squirrels all looked pretty exhausted, ready for a good night's rest knowing they had just accomplished the impossible.

Damn! I sure wish I would have thought to capture the whole thing on video! Would have definitely gone viral.

Twenty-two

Helter Skelter

Humanity appreciates truth about as
much as a squirrel appreciates silver.

~ Vernon Howard

The squirrels' triumphant return from the bird feeder
caper seemed like a celebration of troops returning
from battle. When I arrived back at the community park,
I stopped to make some notes on my observations from
the incident. Relative to my research study, I logged
several key takeaways:

1. The advance planning showed a high degree of
   intelligence, certainly greater than anything I
   could have ever expected.

2. Sam demonstrated considerable trust in Darryl,
   relying on his detailed reconnaissance and
   uncanny observational skills to craft the overall
   operational plan. (the reference to "pilot" training
   notwithstanding…)

3. While Chad did not step up for the lead role that
   would ultimately determine the entire plan's
   success or failure, he became a reluctant
   "volunteer" warrior who was ultimately able to

accomplish the mission, bolstering his self-confidence considerably.

4. The teamwork I observed during the mission was especially inspiring. Each member of the scurry contributed to the success of the task, which I attribute in large part to Sam's leadership and support.

As the group continued to celebrate their amazing accomplishment and after updating my notes, I noticed Sam and Samantha fed Baby before retreating to the nest, while Mama and Emma assumed babysitting duties. I wandered over their way to offer congratulations and observe their interaction with Baby. I was impressed to see Emma smiling and rocking Baby gently in her arms, while Mama looked on approvingly. It was obvious to me that Emma had genuinely enjoyed participating in the bird feeder raid and likely felt a sense of accomplishment and belonging, significant for an adolescent of any species.

Having just eaten, Baby was making all sorts of gurgling and flatulent noises, and Emma added to that symphony by humming what I have to assume was a squirrel lullaby of some sort. Aside from an occasional foul-smelling belch, Baby seemed to be enjoying the attention and was starting to relax.

Mama looked over at Baby and smiled: "Look at that sweet baby. He's grinnin' like a possum eatin' a sweet tater."

As things settled down, Sam motioned for me to follow him back to the stump where we first met so we could continue our conversation. I got the impression he was enjoying the discussion, and I was anxious to continue so I could begin to steer the conversation toward the real issue that precipitated the project. Sam hopped up on the stump as if to let me know he was ready to pick up again where we left off before the bird feeder escapade. Before I could say anything, Sam jumped right in, anticipating my real area of interest.

"You know, Doc, over the past few years, as the community has grown – more houses and more humans – we became concerned at the traffic in the neighborhood. So many cars, golf carts, motorcycles, electric bicycles, and scooters. It's pretty scary when all we want to do is just cross the road."

"I couldn't agree more!"

"As a result, we created a plan to help correct the problem."

"You and your team created a plan to address traffic problems? How are you able to do that?" Something told me this was about to get really interesting!

"Well, as you recently found out firsthand, it involves a *roadway incursion*."

As Sam said "firsthand", he stared straight into my eyes, as though to let me know he was very much aware of my real reason for my research and spending time with him and the group. He waited to see how I would react.

"You mean like the one that almost killed me?"

"I think that's a bit overdramatic, don't you? All you had to do is slow down and hit the brakes. None of us thought you'd swerve and run off the road!"

OMG! They are actually admitting to it! For the life of me, I will never understand why I was unable to control my immediate reactionary outburst.

"By the time I saw you guys in the road, I didn't have a choice!"

"Precisely, Doc. *Precisely*." Sam was again staring straight into my eyes as he continued. It was almost as though I could feel the strength of his emotion. "You know, if the roles were reversed I would have done the same thing."

I had a hard time wrapping my head around that comment, and apparently it showed.

"Yes, if I was behind the wheel and looked up to see you and your family walking across the street, I'm sure I would have reacted the same way."

I have to admit that comment and thought gave me pause. Now, that is not to suggest I actually tried to envision Sam behind the wheel of a car as I was crossing the street with my wife and kids, but I definitely got the message.

As we continued our conversation, I began to understand more about the strategy for these "roadway incursions", but I still needed to find out the *purpose* and ultimate goal for these dangerous escapades. In keeping with my original mission statement, I wanted to learn more about the squirrels' motivation in such risky behavior. For example, with humans I might land on a diagnosis of Intermittent Explosive Disorder (IED), which includes bouts of impulsive, aggressive, and sometimes violent behavior. We often see such behavior in incidents such as road rage, domestic abuse, or violent temper tantrums, but that really does not seem to match what I was seeing in these roadway antics, which appear to me more like dangerous pranks. The question is: are these acts simply playful happenstance or deliberate, premeditated, well-planned missions, as Sam has now suggested? I knew I needed to investigate further, so I was both delighted and apprehensive when Sam offered a rather interesting invitation.

"Tell you what, Doc. Listen, I know why you really came here and what you're trying to do."

"Like I told you, I came to learn more about squirrels – about your species. It's part of my research study."

"Oh, come on, Doc. As Mama would say: 'Don't piss on my leg and tell me it's rainin'!' It seems to me you might be more interested in *roadways* than bird feeders."

Ah, shit! I felt like I just got caught – like my cover was blown and my diabolical plan exposed! I could have chosen to continue to evade and fabricate some cockamamie story, but Sam seemed to be pretty direct and straightforward. Even though I had only known him for a short time, I felt like we had established a mutual sense of trust, so I suppose this was as good a time as any to come clean.

"OK, yes, you got me! I absolutely am interested in learning more about your roadway '*missions*'."

"This afternoon we will be running an operation you might want to see. We usually try to focus on the two-hour window when you humans typically return from work." Once again, the "hooman" pronunciation really cracked me up.

"If you really want to learn more about what we do and why we do it, you need to understand, just as you saw with the bird feeder operation, we always plan *everything*. We never step out into the road without a plan."

"You mean you had a *plan* to kill me the other day?"

"Of course not! We are not trying to kill or injure anyone. Even *you*, Doc!" Sam smiled as he turned away, disappearing behind his erect tail. He scampered over to a log next to park bench. I followed close behind. What is this squirrel up to?

"Here it is." Sam said, reaching his paw inside a hollowed hole in the log, pulling out some type of binder, well-worn and with the pages hanging out haphazardly.

"This is our game plan for what we call *'Brake Dancing'*." My head jerked to stare directly at Sam, who flashed a big buck-toothy squirrel grin. "See what I did there? Get it? '*Brake* Dancing'? It's a *homophone*."

"Thank you, great squirrel master. I *know* what a homophone is!" I said sarcastically. "It's like when some of your guys are over *there* in full view playing with *their* nuts thinking *they're* somehow invisible."

"Good one, Doc. I like that one!" Sam said with a laugh, nodding his head approvingly. He continued: "This is the original playbook Artemis used during my training, and it's the one I use to train every squirrel in our scurry. Artemis used to call it *'Scurry in a Hurry'* – cute, but too old school for my taste and just doesn't work for logoed merchandise." Artemis must have heard his name, because he immediately came over and took a seat behind Sam. The old squirrel is hard of hearing, but he did seem to know when his name entered the conversation.

I'm thinking *"Wait! What the hell did he just say?"* I was speechless (almost).

"You have a playbook? Like, as in sports? Like for playing a *game*? You think dodging cars in the middle of the road is a *game*? *Are you serious?"* I was getting pretty worked up.

"Yes, see here… This is the original pawwritten playbook." (They don't have hands, remember?)

Sam handed me a weather-beaten, leather looking folder with a bunch of tattered pages with markings that appeared to be somehow weirdly scribbled onto the pages. What I saw was absolutely inexplicable and defies logic. I'll give you a hint: how the hell can I be reading an apparently pawwritten squirrel "playbook"? Still don't get it? Here's another hint, then: I don't speak *squirrel*. I have been having conversations with the squirrels *in English*. The playbook I had just been handed was faded and barely legible, *but it was in English*. That begs the question: How the hell do these squirrels know the language? I was a little freaked out, until I reminded myself *I was already freaked out!* My brain was racing trying to sort through so many simultaneous conundrums.

Sam could see the puzzled look on my face. I'm sure I must have looked like a complete dumbshit, trying unsuccessfully to resolve an acute case of cognitive dissonance, attempting to process so many incongruent thoughts creating an almost catatonic state. I just stood there motionless staring at the pages, mouth open, like a young boy unfolding the centerfold of a Playboy magazine for the first time, completely speechless. As my fingers slowly flipped through the pages, I felt like I was a coach in the SFL (*Squirrel Football League*) with my super-secret master playbook.

Sam moved closer and seemed to enjoy my temporary paralysis and astonishment.

"Pretty cool, huh? I think we have added a few new ones over the past few years, but these have been passed on for generations." (Keep in mind that for squirrels, a *generation* is relatively short.)

Regaining my wits, but still fixated on each and every page, I was impressed by the clear and concise play descriptions and the detailed diagrams that accompanied each one. Compared to an actual football playbook, the notable omissions were that the opposing team defense was not depicted, and player positions were not specified. Sam explained that was because the plays were designed such that all participants - male or female, young or old – could fill any or all roles. In thinking about it further, it was all quite obvious: in this case the "opposing team" was *a vehicle driven by a human.* And more importantly, a more accurate analogy would place the squirrels on *defense*, with each play designed as a sort of goal line stand against the oncoming vehicle, preventing it from continuing forward, with a goal of forcing it to a stop. Amazing!

As I slowly thumbed through each page, the playbook seemed to increase in play complexity, with additional participants added and movement patterns becoming more complex. Due to the sensitive and confidential nature of the contents, I was only allowed to review the document before Sam returned it to its secret secure storage location. I was not allowed to take notes, but I remember most of the plays I reviewed. Here are some notable examples:

Solo
One squirrel darts into the road from one direction, typically from the right of the oncoming vehicle(s) and exits the other side.

Changed My Mind
Same as Solo, but the squirrel stops briefly in the middle, then turns and quickly exits from the same direction it entered.

Tandem
Two squirrels, each entering from opposite sides, meet in the middle then exit, returning from the direction they came.

Criss-Cross
Two or more squirrels enter simultaneously from opposite sides, pause briefly in the middle, then continue across to the opposite side.

Possum
Two squirrels enter *well in advance* of oncoming traffic. One lays down and plays dead. The other acts like it's trying desperately to pull the first to safety, before it then jumps up and both run off toward the closest curb.

Cute Baby

Using a child's toy baby stroller and doll, one male and one female squirrel walk upright, pushing the stroller into the street and meet a squirrel coming from the other side, who stops to admire the cute little baby. Seeing the approaching vehicle, all three wave their paws, scream, and run, leaving the stroller unattended in the center of the street.

Helter-Skelter

Three or more squirrels enter the roadway from various directions, stand in the middle, with high-fours, dance moves, and knuckle-bumps, creating total confusion, before exiting at completely random locations.

To say I was completely fascinated would be a huge understatement. As I read through the playbook, Sam explained in great detail how it all worked.

"Our approach is actually pretty simple. Here in this neighborhood, as I'm sure you are already well aware, most of the issues occur when you humans are coming home from work. Since this is a gated neighborhood with one entrance and exit, once traffic passes the entry gate, we choose whichever route: left, straight, or right - is experiencing the most traffic exceeding the posted 15 mph speed limit. For example, all this week, the worst offenders are on the route to the left." I am listening attentively to Sam's explanation of what is about to unfold. Like the bird feeder escapade, it is apparent that Sam and the scurry have done some serious planning. Sam continued:

"Once we have selected a target route, it all starts with Darryl. Over the past year or so, Darryl has compiled research on just any make and model vehicle you can name, and he is especially knowledgeable on those in this neighborhood. He can practically name them by heart."

Recognizing Darryl's relentless quest for perfection worked to the group's advantage, I learned that his role in most missions is *not* to run into the street with the other squirrels. Sam and the others have come to rely on Darryl for "*overwatch*", observing the overall roadway field of play from the branch of a tree, high up and overhanging the street, a good 50 yards from the curve approaching the community tennis court and park. This vantage point allows Darryl an unobstructed view of any oncoming car, and it seems that over time he has used his perch and specific landmarks along the street to estimate the speed of the oncoming vehicle. Keep in mind we're talking about fairly complex estimation calculations, instantaneously completed without the benefit of squirrel laptops, smartphones or other computing power. Based on my observations, I am confident Darryl suffers from a version of *squirrel obsessive compulsive disorder* (SOCD), constantly checking and rechecking his calculations, fearful that an error might prove fatal for the squirrel squad. I suspect that SOCD might well have something to do with the bouts of indecisiveness that often proven fatal to squirrels in roadway interactions with vehicles, but until I could directly observe the mission, that was just speculation. However, after seeing the research and preparation Darryl had done for the feeder heist, I had no reason to doubt he had done his homework for this operation.

"When a vehicle makes a left turn past the gate, Darryl quickly identifies the make and model, then he calculates the speed by counting as the car passes that white mailbox way up there on the right." Sam motioned with his right paw, pointing to the mailbox in front of a large two-story home on the left of the street with what we would consider his index finger. (Gray squirrels have 4 fingers and 5 toes.) "Then he stops counting when the car passes the green mailbox." As Sam pointed in that general direction, he explained that since Darryl had measured the distance between the two mailboxes, he could then calculate the speed of the vehicle. If the car was traveling in excess of 10 miles per hour over the posted speed limit, that vehicle becomes a target.

"Once the target has been acquired, Darryl relays the info to a squirrel on the ground below Darryl's observation perch. For today's mission, that will be

Emma." Sam went on to explain he chose Emma because of the effort she demonstrated during the bird feeder raid, and he thought the responsibility and recognition would further reinforce the importance of everyone pulling their weight. I have to say I was impressed! But I was not sure what the make and model of the vehicle had to do with anything. I had to ask.

"Does it really matter what type of car it is? If they're speeding, they're speeding, right?"

Sam immediately scowled and shook his head. "It matters a LOT! Based on the make and model of the vehicle and the speed at which it is traveling, each has a specified *braking distance*."

Oh shit! I should have thought of that! But then, of course, I am just a lowly human, not some freakin' prodigious *Albert Squirrelstein* savant genius. The importance seemed so obvious once it was pointed out to me by a damn squirrel. How embarrassing!

Sam continued: "When the car gets to a specific marker Darryl has assigned for this mission location, Emma signals Rambo across the street. He acts as a sort of stage manager, queuing up participants like a football coach, with his hand on their shoulder until it's time to send them into the play."

"That's it? You mean they just run out in front of oncoming cars and hope they survive? That's *nuts*!"

Damn! I caught myself just as I heard that one depart my lips.

"Real funny, Doc. We've never heard *that* one before." Sam snapped sarcastically, shaking his head in disgust.

"But they could be killed! Or they could cause an accident and possibly kill someone! Trust me, *I know*!"

"Hey Doc, guess what? If they were going the 15 mph speed limit, nobody would ever get hurt, right? Each of us knows these plays by heart, and we know exactly what we are doing. All the driver has to do is hit the brakes and slow down."

Before I could respond, Artemis stood up and opined: "Back in the day, we could hear a car coming a mile away... heck, we could smell 'em, too! These newfangled contraptions are so damn quiet, now one of us has to be a lookout and warn the rest! I heard tell some cars don't even have engines, anymore! That doesn't make a lick of sense!"

"They're *electric*, old squirrel. They're called EV's." Sam added, as I nodded in agreement.

"Trick? I don't give a damn about their tricks!" Artemis raised his voice. "They don't trick me, no sir! *Trick* engines, ha! They don't fool me. They..." his muttering trailed off as he used an adjacent tree branch to steady himself as he sat back down, having made his point, still mumbling under his breath. As I watched his aging, frail frame, I could only imagine a young Artemis darting out into the road *back in the day,* executing the same plays still being used today.

I wasn't done yet. "Listen, Sam, I don't care if you guys are highly trained, well-rehearsed professionals. Shit happens! What if you're running *Helter Skelter* and two squirrels accidentally bump into each other?" Complete silence. I don't mean no response; there was total, absolute, *complete silence*. Shit! It was like the whole world stopped. So quiet you could hear a fly fart. What the hell was going on? I looked at the other squirrels and noticed none were making eye contact. All we silent and looking straight down at the ground. Was it something I said?

Sam moved closer and put his paw on my hand, as though to comfort me. (He obviously couldn't reach my shoulder - you get the picture.)

"William. His name was Will. Everybody loved Will." I could see the anguish in Sam's face. Out of the corner of my eye, I saw Mama reach out and squeeze Samantha's paw. I braced for the story to come.

"Yes, it was *Helter Skelter*. Damn! I remember that afternoon like it was yesterday." I watched as Rambo, undisputed tough guy of the group, move over to comfort Chad and Darryl, and the three wrapped their arms around each other in a solemn moment. Emma moved over next to Samantha, sobbing noticeably.

"We had just run the baby stroller play, and it worked perfectly! We watched some guy in a Ford Explorer completely freak out, slam on the brakes, and his airbag deployed. Everybody was laughing and running around - pretty amped up. Everything so far had been flawless. So, I called… I called a *Helter Skelter*. We were all so jazzed!" Sam was fidgeting and seemed distraught.

"We have run these plays a hundred times with no problems. Will knew as well as any of us, probably better. He was a real showman, always performing his heart out. I specifically remember the play, *because I was part of it*. It was Will, me, and Samantha. That was before Baby, and Samantha was always so fast and nimble. It all started out just as we planned. Darryl announced a 2022 Hyundai Sonata. Emma made the relay and Rambo gave us the go signal. Samantha and I ran in from the same side, and Will entered from the opposite side of the street. Samantha started with freeze frame poses, adding a cartwheel as she moved toward the center. I started with some traditional breakdance moves – leg rotations, then a backspin up to a headspin. I remember Will started with his trademark robot moves – he was so good with those! Then he turned around, stood on his hind legs and moonwalked backwards toward me, just as Samantha cartwheeled by and I was popping back up on my feet from a headspin. There was no way Will could see us as he glided backwards, and he bumped into Samantha. It was no big deal, but he was startled and lost his footing for just a split second. That's all it took."

I watched the looks of anguish and despair on the faces of the squirrels, raw emotion reliving what must have been a truly horrific event. Sam paused and shook his head, then continued the story.

"Samantha went back toward Rambo, who caught her as she bounded up on the curb. I ran toward Will, reaching out my hand to pull him up off the pavement. The look in his eyes! I'll never forget it. He knew that even a second's hesitation would mean both of us would not make it, and he waved me off, scrambling to his feet on his own as I scampered by. I barely made it to the curb, and when I turned around…well, it was too late. The car braked hard and swerved to the left, just like you did, but apparently the tires had a lot of wear, and the car skidded, taking Will with it. A guy got out of the car and seemed pretty rattled, then he saw Will motionless on the pavement with blood… it was a very disturbing scene." I stepped over to Sam and placed my hand on his shoulder.

"I am so sorry, Sam. That is horrible. That is a terrible way to go. At least he was there with his friends doing what he loved doing." Sam wiped away a tear.

"It was a freakin' Hyundai. A Hyundai!" He shook his head in disgust. "He deserved so much better. A Corvette, maybe. A Porsche. Instead, it was a Hyundai with bad tires. Oh my god!"

As Sam tried in vain to control his anger and heartache, I watched as each squirrel slowly walked toward him, circling him in a comforting, collective hug. Only sobs broke the respectful silence. Then an interesting happened. Chad unexpectedly broke from the huddle and spoke loudly.

"I tell you what. When it's my time to go, it won't be a damn Hyundai! No way!" Caught by surprise, the others turned to see normally shy Chad continuing his proclamation.

"Nah, I'm thinking maybe a Lexus like that pilot lady, or one of those new Audis." The comment elicited a few giggles, and soon the group joined in.

Darryl immediately weighed in: "Ha! When it's my time, I'd prefer a BMW, thank you very much!"

Samantha offered: "Make mine a Mercedes, please; a shiny *new one* would be nice!"

Emma wouldn't be outdone, and moved to the front, acting out a dismissive, aristocratic princess paw-wave motion: "I much prefer a Ferrari…no, wait…I think a Lamborghini. Lovely!"

Rambo stepped up, dwarfing the rest, and snapped to attention. "I say bring on a Hummer! Let's see what you got!" At this point, the mood was beginning to turn, and I saw smiles for the first time in a while. Darryl managed a grin and looked straight at Rambo. "Just your luck my friend, some stupid fool would try to run you over with a Volkswagen!"

Seemingly out of nowhere, Mama's voice rang out: "A Volkswagen's just gonna bounce off that big guy, bless his heart."

Sam joined the chorus: "Yes, they're going to need an 18-wheeler for Rambo!" The entire group erupted in laughter, which apparently either startled or woke up Artemis.

"What? There ain't no semi-trucks on these streets! Back in the day, we'd have all sorts of big clunkers and muscle cars come through. You gonna have to settle for one of those smiley face Amazon delivery vans!" Rambo doubled over, completely hysterical. And, oh yeh…the commotion definitely woke up Baby, who immediately offered his unique, acrid, blood curdling shriek, followed by an especially odiferous cloud. This caused the group to cover their ears, hold their noses, cough, choke, and laugh – all at the same time. Eventually, Sam looked over at me, regaining his composure.

"Tell you what, Doc. I think it's time for us to do what we do." He turned to face the group.

"OK, everybody. Listen up. Doc here had a little mishap the other day." (Muffled laughter.)

"Why don't we show him what we do and why we do it?" The scurry erupted with cheers and applause.

"OK, let's head to the street." Sam motioned for me to follow. I want to learn more about what motivates these squirrels to risk their lives in roadways. This should be interesting!

Twenty-three

Brake Dancing

Squirrels are just rats with good publicity.

~ Garrison Wynn

We arrived at the street just as folks living in the neighborhood were coming home from work. Just as Sam explained, he had already made assignments for the "mission", and the team was already moving into their respective positions. I watched as Emma gave Darryl a high-four, and he turned to scamper up a tall pine tree near the street and chose an overhanging branch that afforded an unobstructed view up the street toward the entrance to the community. Emma took her position beneath the tree, close to the curb so she could relay Darryl's information to Rambo, who was busy going over the first "play". To get started, Sam had called a *Criss-Cross*, with Samantha and Chad assuming positions on opposite sides of the street. Mama was watching Baby for the mission and stayed out of sight with Sam and Artemis just behind Rambo, while I found a spot to hide on the opposite of the street. I didn't want anyone in the neighborhood to see me "observing" what was about to happen, so I hid between a hibiscus shrub and a boxwood hedge, like a rank amateur in a hunting blind. From my location I could see several hundred yards up the street and had a direct line of sight with Darryl's tree branch position, as well as Emma and Rambo.

Sam called out a final check and got a paws-up response (they don't have thumbs, ya' know) from Darryl, Emma, and Rambo. The scene was set, players in place, and we waited for the next vehicle coming through the gate and turning in our direction. To say I was nervous and anxious is an understatement, and I felt my heartbeat quicken with anticipation. Just as I was dealing with my newfound hyperawareness, I heard the first call from Darryl, a high-pitched whistling noise, which made sense since gray squirrels hear at higher frequencies and over a much greater range than humans. The whistle was immediately followed by a staccato burst of very specific data: "2023 red Chevy Equinox, female + 1". I later learned that the "female + 1" referred to the driver and one passenger and was assured that whenever children in car seats were observed, the vehicle would be allowed to pass without incident. That not being the case with the Equinox, I watched intently as the squirrels prepared for action.

While I could not see whatever landmark Darryl was using as a cue for when the car passed by, I clearly heard his call of "Now!", which Emma immediately flashed to Rambo with a quick downward arm motion. Now I could see the Equinox headed our way, and seconds later Rambo gave Chad a tap on the shoulder and slight nudge, sending him in like a football player coming in from the sideline. Simultaneously, Samantha entered the road from the opposite side, and each did a sort of stutter-step dance move toward the center of the street, with the car fast approaching, all the while. I involuntary clenched my hands, as I watched Chad and Samantha meet in the middle of the road, quickly exchange double high-fours, and continue across to the opposite side and hop up onto the curb, turning around to watch for any effect on the vehicle. From my vantage point looking at the driver's side of the vehicle, when the squirrels reached the center of the street, I definitely saw the car jerk abruptly, but only momentarily, then continue forward as the driver glanced briefly to her left just after Samantha and Chad had exited the roadway. Whew! Seemed pretty close to me!

The squirrels were ecstatic, with cheers and congratulations all around. I wanted to cross the street to discuss what had just taken place with Sam, but before I could emerge from my hiding spot, Darryl sounded off again. "Blue 2024 Audi A4, male." Sam immediately called *Changed My Mind* and tapped Rambo, who flashed a big grin, clearly delighted to join the fun. After just a few seconds, I could see the shiny new blue Audi headed our way. I looked up to watch Darryl, who appeared to be counting with downward arm motions, until yelling "Now!" Emma relayed the signal, and Rambo ambled out onto the road. He scampered briskly to the center, stood up, put his paw on his chin and cocked his head as though he forgot something, then turned and ran back to the curb. Just as Rambo was making his move to return and evade the oncoming vehicle, I saw the driver's startled look, as he gripped the wheel tightly and slammed on the brakes. The car shuddered but did not veer off, coming to a stop just a few feet from where Rambo had stood just seconds earlier. The driver glanced over toward the curb, where Rambo had slipped into the bushes next to the tennis court – quite the disappearing act!

The Audi continued down the road, the driver no doubt shaken by the episode. After the car passed by, Sam and the others reemerged, and Rambo popped up out of the bushes, making a grand entrance to the cheers of the group and bowing to his fans. Sam looked up toward Darryl and flashed the universal time-out sign, which Darryl acknowledged and then retreated down from his perch. With a break in the action, I poked my head through the hedge and walked to the other side of the street to join Sam and the group. All seemed pleased with the results, and I followed Sam, who had crawled up onto a bench inside the tennis court fence, away from the others. It was the perfect opportunity to have a frank conversation about what I had just observed.

Sam jumped right in: "So, what did you think?"

"Impressive. A little *scary*, but impressive." I wanted to ease into it and didn't want to be "that guy".

"Now you can see that we are always well prepared, and we never want anyone to get hurt, including us!" He was clearly proud of the accomplishment and probably expected I would feel the same way.

"Well, I have to say it was exciting, but I am really concerned about the risk, both for your team and the unsuspecting drivers."

"I appreciate your concern, and I hope now you can appreciate that we are not crazy, suicidal creatures with some morbid death wish. Please understand we are relying not only on our play execution and practice regimen, but also our research and intelligence regarding these vehicles you humans drive."

"What do you mean? What does that have to do with what I just witnessed?"

"Everything! Darryl is a gifted researcher and master statistician. I guarantee you he knows more about your cars than the drivers do! For example, he knows that the older models don't have the advanced crash avoidance systems and autonomous emergency braking found in new cars today. So, he factors that into his calculations for the *go* signal. We know that the newer models have all sorts of sensors to provide drivers advance warning, and that helps reduce the risk for the drivers and for us."

"That sounds very sophisticated, and I am certainly impressed with Darryl's incredible research, skills, and intellect…"

Sam turned toward me: "It sounds like there is a 'but' coming." I smiled.

"*But*, I'm not sure you have allowed for two things that could prove disastrous. The first is simply what we humans call *human error*. To me that actually has *two* meanings for your missions. What we will now call *'squirrel error'* could be any number of seemingly minor mistakes, unintentional and often accidental, that can occur even with the most rigorous planning and practice. Rambo makes his turn but slips and falls, just for split-second. Two players see a car swerving and accidentally bump into each other in the center of the street. And *human* error is still always there for the *drivers* – sun in their eyes, distracted driving, slow reaction time."

"True, and we know those risks are there. *WE* live with risk every day: predators, falling from broken branches…"

"But the second thing you may not be considering is that even the newest cars with the very latest in crash avoidance technologies – radar, lasers, cameras, and sophisticated algorithms - even the best cutting-edge stuff, they are primarily designed to detect and react to other motor vehicles, pedestrians, and major obstructions."

Sam nodded. "And your point?"

"That list doesn't include *squirrels*." Ouch! I knew that would hurt! I let it sink in for a moment before continuing. "So you are really relying on each and every driver, hoping they all will see you in time, react immediately, and that reaction will not result in harm to any squirrel or human. That's a pretty big leap of faith, don't you think?" I watched as Sam heard my comments and seemed to be processing them before responding.

"Well, I guess I never thought of it quite that way."

"Speaking from my very painful personal experience, and now after seeing how it all works from your perspective, I am completely confident your team performed precisely according to their training. I admit I had a lot on my mind that day, but I definitely saw you guys in the middle of the road and reacted as quickly as I could. You may not believe it, but on behalf of all of us humans, I assure you *none of us would purposely want to murder any squirrels*! Well, at least any *sane* human." Sam chuckled and shook his head. He started to speak, but before he could get a word out, I held up my hand to let him know I was not finished.

"I can tell you that in my case, I was absolutely terrified! When I hit the brakes, I felt like my foot was going to drive the pedal right through the floorboard!

I was scared to death I might have acted too late, and that's why my reaction was to swerve hard to the left top avoid hitting any of you. My foot was still on the brake when my car jumped the curb and hit the tree."

"And we all want you to know we are really sorry about that." Sam slowly bowed and shook his head.

"Thanks, but the point is my effort to avoid hurting any of you could have killed me! I didn't get an avoidance warning until I swerved toward the curb, and then it was too late."

This is a good time to pause to consider the scene at this precise moment. I was standing on the side of a street in my neighborhood, one I travel virtually every day. Only at this moment in time, I was with a group of squirrels, talking to their leader and calmly explaining why running out into the middle of the road in front of oncoming cars is not in the best interest of the squirrel species or human drivers. *Seriously.* Just something to think about...

Sam looked very serious and pensive. I could tell my words had an impact, and I wanted to make sure I didn't pull any punches or appear in any way apologetic for my actions. Let's face it, I can't order Sam to cease and desist or threaten to exterminate him and his scurry. This was very much a civilized man-to-squirrel discussion, with a goal of convincing Sam and his cadre that we all need to find a better way to address areas of mutual concern. In this case that meant first figuring out a plan to bring awareness of the danger speeding vehicles present not only to community residents, children, and pets, but also to wildlife that may intrude on the streets. In our neighborhood, that certainly includes squirrels, but also deer, wild turkey, sand hill crane, gopher tortoise, raccoon, and a variety of other animal species.

After what seemed like several minutes, Sam turned and stood upright directly in front of me.

"You know, Doc, I have to admit you've raised some good points. I guess we have been looking at this issue only from our perspective. It sounds like we have our work cut out for us, then."

"I just think there may be a better way to get your message across."

"Well, what do you propose? I'm all ears." As Sam made the comment, he made sure I could see his ears doing all sorts of weird contortions, just as they would do whenever a squirrel stops to evaluate potential danger.

Thus began a more than hour-long discussion between me and a squirrel. Sam seemed genuinely interested in hearing my ideas, and I explained that, like any good marketing campaign, it all begins with capturing the attention of the target audience. Since in this case we are dealing with an *issue* and not a *product*, we would need to create awareness of the issue in the minds of drivers. I explained it to Sam this way:

"You know, a few minutes ago you said you had only considered the issue *from your perspective*." Sam nodded his agreement.

"That's exactly what we want *human drivers* to do! We want anyone who drives a vehicle to be acutely aware that the more development encroaches on animal habitat, the more important it is to recognize we share the roadways with a variety of species, including squirrels."

As I said the word "squirrels", Sam was saying it simultaneously, smiling and nodding in agreement.

"And something else you said earlier gave me the perfect answer."

"It did? I mean, *I did*?"

"Trust me, marketing to humans is all about psychology and brand awareness, creating something to communicate with drivers to demonstrate the importance of the issue – with images and a catchy slogan to grab their attention."

"That makes sense, but what did I say that could help accomplish that?

"You were pretty proud of the moniker you created for your roadway incursions, remember."

"Of course! We call them *Brake Dancing*, a play on words."

"Exactly! How about this: we need a very concise, catchy phrase to capture and communicate the issue. *'Slow down for squirrels'* just isn't going to cut it."

Sam protested: "But that's exactly what we want them to do!"

"True, true. But it lacks punch. It's not *memorable*. You know what *is*? Are you ready?"

"Come on, Doc! Spit it out!"

"It's simple, really. Most great marketing taglines are. Imagine a picture of a cute, lovable squirrel in the middle of the road with oncoming traffic. The tagline: '*Give me a brake!*' Short, sweet, and to the point! It's perfect!"

Sam smiled and nodded. "I've got to hand it to you, Doc. I really like it!"

"Presented with the right image, it could be very powerful and memorable. I think it has potential for other variations: *Give us a brake! We need a brake! We deserve a brake!* I see tremendous marketability and plenty of opportunities for merchandising."

Sam was enthusiastic: "Much better than a lame *'Squirrel Crossing'* sign, for sure!" We both laughed at the thought, and I immediately pictured a typical yellow caution sign with a squirrel silhouette, not very original.

"I'm just glad to know you're not *homophone-bic*!" I watched as he processed the punchline and erupted into laughter, a very satisfying response.

"That's a good one, Doc! Cracks me up!"

"Really? Not too *nutty* for you?" Sam's head jerked around, displaying a mock stern face.

"OK, don't push your luck. What do we need to do?"

I mean, it's not like we just came up with the best slogan of all time. It's clearly not on par with Nike's *Just do it!, America Runs on Dunkin'*, or *What's in your wallet?* But for our current challenge, it'll do just fine. If we can create a plan that incorporates our mutual best interests, we just might be onto something.

Sam was so interested and energized in talking more about the possibility of squirrels and humans coming together to solve the age-old *Why did the squirrel not quite cross the road?"* mystery, we sat for hours brainstorming and fashioning a plan. As I looked around the park, I realized it was starting to get dark. I think Sam would have kept going for hours, but I was dead tired and felt we had accomplished quite a lot.

"Hey, Sam. Tell you what. I don't want to lose our momentum here, but we've been at it for a while, and I could use a break. If it's OK with you, I'm going to grab a brief catnap, and we can hit it again in just a bit." Sam nodded and even though Samantha and the rest of the scurry were some distance from where we were in the park, the minute I said "*cat*nap", I immediately heard Baby squealing. His bellowing was accompanied by a loud fart, followed by what felt like a ground tremor. What the hell is up with that kid?

I eventually found myself getting incredibly sleepy, so I found a soft spot on the grass and guess I must have finally nodded off. A lot to dream about...

Twenty-four

The Wake-Up

You can't be suspicious of a tree or
accuse a bird or a squirrel of subversion
or challenge the ideology of a violet.

~ Hal Borland

I vaguely remember waking up – at least trying to, but my eyelids wouldn't cooperate. It was like they were stuck together with *Gorilla Glue* and refused to respond to my commands. What's up with that? Odd…they had always worked before. Why do I have a headache? What time is it, anyway? Am I home in my own bed or being held captive by some sinister, evil *Lord of Darkness*? What the hell is going on here? Yes, even psychologists can experience an unexpected anxiety attack or major paranoia induced psychotic episode.

Convinced that I had been the victim of some sort of lame eyelid gluing prank or somehow sucked into a cosmic black hole, I struggled to reach for my phone but only managed to knock what felt and sounded like a plastic water bottle onto the floor. This failure prompted me to yell for help from my wife – more like a *yelp*, actually, or a sad whimper.

"Honey, can you help me?" No response. OK, let's take it up an octave and increase the decibel level. "**Honey?**" Wait a few seconds… "**Hello?**"

After what seemed like an eternity and as I was completely exasperated and flailing about blindly, I heard what sounded like the garage door closing. I tried one more time.

"Honey? Is that you? I could use your help."

Eventually, Christy responded: "Yes, I'll be right there after I put away the groceries."

Well, isn't that just great? I'm laying here completely helpless and apparently going blind, and nobody shares the urgency of my obviously life-threatening situation. OK, no problem. Don't worry about me. I will just sit here in this dark, endless void. I will no longer cry out expecting the world to acknowledge my plight. I am a man, damnit! Man up, buddy! Show the world you're down but not done. Let them know you can survive this calamity. Say it!

I responded softly: "Thank you, sweetie. Whenever you're done."

After what seemed like an eternity, Christy arrived at our bedroom door.

"Sorry, honey. How are you feeling? You went out like a light!"

"Like a light? Hey, speaking of light, can you help me? I swear my eyelids feel like they're welded together. Could you grab me a warm washcloth or something? I sat up in the bed, motioning haphazardly toward my face.

"Of course!" She immediately brought back a warm facecloth and helped maneuver my hand to use it to wipe my eyes, as she sat next to me on the bed.

She then explained her theory on what may have caused my current predicament.

"When we got home from the hospital, just like the doctor warned, you were still really sore and a little bit loopy. I know you were hurting, but the doctor was very specific about the pain meds and sleep aid. I don't think the dose they gave you through the IV had even worn off, but you were pretty wired and said you had to get some rest. I told you to be careful, *but no* – Mr. Clinical Psychologist insisted you knew what you were doing."

"I said that?" I lowered my voice and pressed the warm cloth to one eye, then the other. Both were crusted over; most likely I was extremely dehydrated.

"You said *a lot* of shit! Most of it didn't make sense, and you mixed up the instructions for the meds. You took two of the sleeping pills, instead of just one, plus one of the high-dose pain meds."

"Crap! I did all that? I really don't remember..." At this point I was completely embarrassed, still wiping my eyes with the washcloth. I was beginning to slowly pry the eyelids apart, like the seal on some frustrating Ziploc bag. Everything was still blurry and dim, but slowly improving.

"Yep, *Mr. I Know Better* let everyone know you just wanted to crash. And crash you did. You stopped making sense around 9 last night."

"Oh, shit! I'm sorry!"

"By about 9:15 you were virtually comatose. You know what that means, right?"

"Of course, I know what that means!" I snapped. "I *said* I was sorry. Yesterday was a pretty tough day, ya' know." OK, I realize that was a pretty lame play for some sympathy. Trust me, *it didn't work.*

Christy responded: "You know what sweetheart? It was a tough day for *all* of us."

"Wait, what time is it, anyway?"

"It's almost 11." I thought wow, I slept in for a change! I'm usually up by 6:30, but I was grateful for the additional hours. I was still a little groggy and just starting to focus.

"I guess I needed the rest. Thank you for taking care of me."

"You're welcome. I was really concerned about you." She smiled and held my hand, this time without crushing it. I decided I would take the opportunity to share my exciting news.

"You know, when I was at the park this morning, I…"
Christy recoiled, obviously startled, and interrupted.
"At the park? Don't be silly, you doofus!"

"But I had an *amazing* morning at the park. You won't believe what happened! I *really* want to tell you about it. I thought maybe we could do breakfast."

Christy just stared at me with an astonished look on her face. She let go of my hand, stood up, and backed away, as though I had just told her I had contracted COVID, or something worse. What the hell was going on? Her demeanor changed, and now she looked angry.

"Look, it's 11 o'clock, so don't mess with me, alright? You've been completely out of it ever since you got back from the hospital yesterday. You haven't moved in that bed since then, it's late at night, and I'm ready to call it a day."

"Wait! What? *Night*? What do you mean, *night*?"

"It's after 11 o'clock at night, I've been worried about you, I'm exhausted, and I just need to go to bed, OK? Whatever you need to tell me can wait until morning. Don't forget you have a follow-up appointment with the doctor tomorrow."

I was completely confused and speechless, which I'm sure suited my wife just fine. I stood there motionless for what seemed like an eternity, trying in vain to process what the hell was going on. Had I really been in bed and virtually out of it since I left the hospital? That didn't make sense. I walked to the window and checked my phone for the time. Christy was right, it's definitely late at night. Wait, I know I was in the park with the squirrels yesterday…or was it this morning? But how could I have such vivid memories of my conversations with Sam? I very clearly saw that amazing bird feeder escapade. I remember every detail; it was pretty incredible! But how could I have been there to observe that and not remember getting back here, waking up in my bed? Is Christy just messing with me? She loves a good joke, but she seemed really serious and pissed off. Something is not right. I am positive I watched Sam and the other squirrels running synchronized *brake dancing* plays in the street, right? Didn't I? That was yesterday, wasn't it? What the hell was wrong with me? I needed to lie down. I grabbed a beer and the meds from the hospital. I kept telling myself I needed to just calm down and figure this whole thing out. There has to be a logical explanation. At least I sure hoped so. I'm pretty sure they told me two of the blue pills…I didn't want to wake Christy and decided I would just close my eyes on the couch for a few minutes.

The next morning Christy let me know she would be driving me to the doctor's office. My take on her adamant insistence: it was most likely a concern for *her own* personal safety. As we pulled out of the driveway, she turned right, which is *not* toward the subdivision exit. I started to say something, but she raised her hand in my direction, such as a parent might do to warn a child that talking was neither required nor advisable at that instant. I swallowed my question, then realized she was instead headed in the direction of the community park - you know, the one where "the incident" occurred. As we crossed the last intersection before the park entrance, I saw what appeared to be something in the road ahead. I didn't choose to say anything… well, you know, because of the whole *"talk to the hand"* thing and the fact that just approaching the park made me anxious. I wanted to avoid any flashbacks, and as I maintained a focus on the road I saw movement, but now the road was clear. What?

My wife had now purposely slowed down, probably her sweet, thoughtful way of forcing me to relive the accident and once again experience the pain and suffering I had caused. Doing so in slow motion might allow me to more accurately reflect on the errors of my way. But what the heck is *that*? What did my now unglued eyes behold? There, completely out of the roadway and positioned along the curb were the squirrels! As we moved closer, one by one they stood erect with their tails positioned high and straight, almost like a salute. Before I could say anything, Christy had noticed them, as well.

"Look, sweetie! The squirrels saw us coming and moved out of the road. Look how they are all lined up there on the side." She smiled broadly. "How cute! I can't imagine how these adorable little animals could ever be a problem."

I was stunned! Have you ever bitten your lip so hard, it bleeds? But don't you dare cry out! No, you must not show weakness! Can this woman not see that these devious creatures were only doing this to taunt me? Or worse, maybe they were purposely creating a distraction to see if they can cause Christy to be distracted and suffer a fate similar to my own? I bet they are just waiting until the last split-second for Sam to call some new trick play. That had to be it, right?

I was totally speechless as we slowly approached the park walkway entrance. The scene was a surreal mashup, a cross between a supportive and waving parade audience, passing presidential motorcade, and solemn funeral procession, all mixed together. Weird, I know.

I remained silent as we slowly moved past the park entrance, but my eyes were locked like laser beams on the faces of each squirrel. I was cautious not to flatter myself by thinking their thoughtful parting gesture was in any way a tribute to our time together. Perhaps it was the squirrels' way of bidding a final farewell, probably assuming my wife was loving and caring enough to finally have me committed for psychiatric treatment. Just as the car started to regain speed and move away from the park entrance, I saw one squirrel move out into the center of roadway, but only one. I swiveled my head to face the rear of the vehicle. Through the rear window I clearly saw… it was Baby, standing in the middle of the road, tail erect, and his little paws extended high, offering a two-pawed equivalent of a double middle finger salute.

I felt my anger morph into compassion and thought to myself: "That little squirrel-of-a-bitch!" as a car passed by in the opposite direction. Funny, I didn't recall Baby being directly involved in any brake dancing plays. Maybe it was time for him to step up and take his place with the others? Or maybe, just maybe he was still pissed off that I hadn't made good on the promise I made to his mom to take him fishing sometime at the pond. Regardless, just as I turned back around, I could swear I heard the sound of screeching tires behind us.

Christy smiled and reached out to hold my hand. "You OK?"
"Absolutely! Never better."

At the doctor's office my follow-up visit was mostly unremarkable, although he did tell me that sometimes with a concussion, combined with the lingering effects of the pain meds and sleep aids, might include adverse side effects like blurred vision, irregular heartbeat, and in rare cases, hallucinations.

And so the story of my research into the motivation of squirrels comes to an end...or does it?

Epilogue

The Aftermath

When I see squirrels or other animals venturing
into a roadway, I immediately slow down.
I think they deserve a *brake*.

~ Ron Cook

I realize many of you are no doubt wondering what has happened since my encounter with these marvelous, mischievous creatures. I realize there continues to be a degree of controversy regarding my version of the events that transpired, and I can only assure you the details are *precisely* what I am *absolutely 100% positive* actually occurred… or at least pretty sure. Following the early release of the book and associated media frenzy, I am sure you can appreciate that I have been careful to distance myself, at least temporarily, from the scurry and the community park. Yes, I am aware that the squirrels did initially give a series of interviews promoting the upcoming *Nature Channel* documentary on my work, and the credits clearly acknowledge each squirrel's contribution to the production. Some have gone so far as to participate in the rounds of popular Sunday morning news talk shows, where they were quick to refute rumors of bribes or influence peddling. Gifts I may or may not have given the scurry and individual members were strictly tokens of gratitude, and any claims or suggestions they were somehow "payoffs" or "hush money" are simply nuts.

On a positive note, the *Give me a brake!* and *Give us a brake!* taglines proved so successful, the messaging garnered the attention of several prominent national animal rights groups, which helped facilitate fundraising efforts that ultimately resulted in raising well over $45 million. Those donations were further amplified as the program caught the attention of corporate sponsors. Several of the same CEOs who initially thought the whole concept was completely nuts and passed up the opportunity are now enthusiastically supporting it. While they originally thought the plan was not what it was cracked up to be, ironically they represent brands you probably recognize, such as *Planters* and *Blue Diamond*. World renowned advertising agency *Ogilvy* created the national campaign in the US, which quickly spread to other countries. The US rollout featured Emma as the face of the campaign, with a beautiful and captivating photo session resulting in a demure, sympathy evoking image, the polar opposite of Emma's more provocative and extremely lucrative *OnlySquirrelFans* monetized page offerings. The campaign included nationwide outdoor advertising, focusing on those markets with the greatest squirrel populations and more generally those with the highest incidence of accidents involving animals. On my recent flight to Los Angeles, I had to laugh when the in-flight magazine included a feature story about how the campaign originated. Then, as I was chatting with a fellow passenger, the flight attendant placed a small bag of *Planters* peanuts with Emma's picture prominently on the packaging, reminding us animals need a *brake*. Too funny!

In addition to the national ad campaign, those funds also supported community programs through local contribution matching campaigns, and that grassroots support and volunteers helped raise awareness in individual neighborhoods. Local clubs and social media groups adopted the tagline, as well as a new slogan *"We have families, too!"*. Not surprisingly, many community groups have added their own local flavor, which has resulted in an avalanche of pretty lame and occasionally humorous local taglines. Some of my personal favorites:

- Human, slow your roll! (in audio clips, it's *hooman*)
- Are you *nuts*? Slow down!
- Don't *tread* on me!

And yes, in case you are wondering, squirrels now have their very own yellow and black squirrel crossing silhouette caution signs!

As far as our local squirrel scurry is concerned, Sam still leads the group, but he has reduced his direct involvement with bird feeder and roadway incursion escapades, because Samantha is expecting again. Baby has grown and is still as ornery as ever, but guess who stepped up to take Baby under his wing (or arm, tail - whatever)? Chad! Sam asked Chad to join him in teaching Baby the requisite squirrelhood training, including scamper skills, basic foraging, advanced branch jumping, and…well, having "that talk" about *the squirrels and the bees*, if you know what I mean. That is certainly quite a step for a squirrel who not that long ago had to be "volunteered" for the starring role in a mission! Now that Baby has grown and can speak for himself, he insists on being called "Bruce". I am not sure where that name came from, but I'm told he does watch a lot of martial arts movies on *Nutflix* and is often seen in the park practicing various moves he has seen on *SquirrelTube,* with Rambo as his coach and mentor. Apparently he likes to show off by breaking multiple branches simultaneously with his front and rear paws, but his favorite stunt is crushing various types of nuts with his forehead. While I have not personally spoken with the young squirrel, I've heard that puberty has seen his voice drop from a whiny, shrill soprano to a low, deeply resonant low-end bass, reminiscent of *Darth Vader*.

Sam is obviously extremely proud of the scurry's contribution to animal safety and takes great pride in each squirrel's continued personal involvement. While he is certainly not contemplating retirement anytime soon, it is clear Sam is committed to maintaining a better work/life balance, especially with another baby on the way. However, he remains very involved as an active participant and coach for the *Bird Feeder Pole Challenge* league, which occasionally involves travel outside of the area. Apparently, with the new interest and influence from corporate sponsorship and increased media coverage, the league rules were recently changed to specifically prohibit participation by so-called *flying squirrels*. I was surprised Sam didn't take kindly to my tongue in cheek suggestion that he might want to consider referring to the league participants as *pole dancers*. Personally, I thought it was pretty damn funny! (*Brake dancing*, bird feeder poles…you get it, right?) Sam also enjoys spending quality time with his many grandsquirrels, playing tail-tag with them in the park and spoiling them with what he refers to as *"luxury tours"*, foraging for treats below the feeder poles of the community's more affluent residents.

I was pleased to hear recently that Artemis was still alive and kicking, which absolutely sets him up for potentially becoming the world's oldest living squirrel! Due to his limited mobility, failing eyesight, and hearing loss, Sam and Mama made the difficult but necessary decision to move Artemis to a squirrel assisted living facility, *Squirreltopia*. Sam tells me Artemis has already become somewhat of a celebrity there and has used his notoriety to his advantage with the squirrel nurses and support staff, especially the females. Sam told me that when he recently visited Artemis at the Sanctuary, the manager told Sam that keeping an eye on Artemis was quite a challenge, citing a recent example of a conversation Artemis had with the facility's attending physician, a distinguished squirrel general practitioner, specializing in elder care. The conversation was from a recent wellness check.

"Artemis, your vital signs are fine. Do you have any difficulty sleeping?"

"Well, Doc, it's quiet as a library here after lights-out, so yeh, I'm sleeping fine."

"Eating well? Any digestive issues?"

"I wouldn't call the food here 'eating well', but no, I don't have any issues."

"Any problems urinating or moving your bowels?"

"No, I pee every morning at around 6 and take a shit around 6:30."

"Good, I'm glad to hear that!"

"Problem is, Doc - I don't wake up until 7!"

As previously noted, Emma has split her time and attention between modeling for the squirrel campaign and her more provocative fans-only monetized channels and content. She hosts a popular nationally syndicated podcast on squirrel fashion trends and grooming called *Tall Tails*. Following her modeling work and inclusion in the national ad campaign, she appeared on the cover of *CoverSquirrel* magazine and recently announced the launch of her own line of *CoverSquirrel* cosmetics, including her favorite vibrant paw nail polish colors, tail powders, brushes, and accessories. Further brand extensions include a line of fragrances, and Emma conducted extensive research into the role of squirrel pheromones as potential sexual attractants. Since squirrel males are already highly promiscuous (as noted here in earlier chapters) and certainly not in need of further arousal, Emma's idea was to create a specially formulated pheromone-infused fragrance to *tamp down* the males' perpetually horny state. She calls it *Leave Me the Fuh Cologne*.

Mama has become a well-known author, publishing a popular cookbook featuring recipes for cooking with various types of nuts. It's called *Feelin' Nutty* and has received glowing critical reviews, propelling it to the top ten recommended list on Amazon. Word in squirrel world is that Mama might be signed to do a new cooking show on the *Squirrelicious Channel*. It would focus on baking and of course include recipes from her book, but would also feature various squirrel home cook celebrities. In addition, Mama recently published an illustrated collection of her favorite heartwarming sayings, simply entitled *Bless Her Heart*. With Samantha nest-bound with a new baby on the way, Mama has stepped up as Emma's unofficial manager and is often on the road with Emma promoting both the *Give Me a Brake!* campaign and Emma's cosmetic and fragrance lines. As Mama describes her role: "The first time we did a major presentation for potential sponsors on Madison Avenue, I was as nervous as a long-tailed cat in a roomful of rocking chairs! My job is to make sure that pretty little face is always on schedule and stays out of trouble, 'cause if she ain't she knows I'm gonna jerk her bald, bless her heart."

Rambo was so impressed by the overwhelming response for the roadway safety initiative from the local community, he approached the neighborhood watch organizations in the surrounding area with a proposal for collaboration on other safety and security issues, something he calls *Squirrel Force*. (I tried to convince him to go with *Squirrel Squad*, but he gave me a very stern look and growled, so I backed off.) His plan includes having *Squirrel Force* members act as a sort of community *overwatch* from strategically selected tree branch positions, communicating suspicious activities to the community entry gate and security patrol officers via prearranged signals. Much like the roadway incursion playbook, Rambo created a complete squirrel/human sign language, allowing the squirrel sentries to function as a type of early warning system to pass reports between themselves and security personnel below. His efforts earned Rambo a certificate of commendation from our local sheriff's department and more importantly, the program has already grown to neighboring states. Even more exciting, Rambo was recently approached by a well-known Hollywood producer about a possible role in a new action-adventure film, *Squirrelpocalypse*. As I understand it, the holdup is that the producer is having a hard time explaining to Rambo why he can't use his real name in the film. (I also heard Rambo had previously turned down a starring role in *Squirrelmageddon* and had been offered a spot in an off-Broadway production of *Squirrel on a Hot Tin Roof*.)

I was excited to hear Chad was able to reunite with his mom. Apparently she got word of his achievements within the scurry and contacted him in an effort to reconcile. You will recall Chad's mom was a well-known squoozy (squirrel floozy) who was known for late night partying and hitting the nut juice pretty hard. In fact, Sam and others were concerned that Chad may have suffered with fetal nut syndrome as a result of his mom's apparent addiction. In addition to pounding the juice, she was busted for bootlegging acorn dust (the street name for a powerful nut/mushroom concoction) and was so out of it she never even reacted to Chad's disappearance or made any effort to find him. She eventually hit bottom and checked herself into rehab, and Chad was pleased to hear she had more recently been clean and sober for more than a year.

Their reunion underneath the same oak tree where Chad's fall from the nest almost cost him his life was both awkward and poignant. Seeing his mom finally getting her act together was heartwarming for Chad, but in his heart he knew that Sam's scurry was his real family. His mom seemed genuinely proud of the squirrel Chad had become and managed a laugh as Chad recounted the details of the infamous bird feeder mission. After just a few hours of stories (that whole *chipmunk thing* was not discussed) and pictures of the siblings Chad had never had a chance to know, his mother left his life again, this time with a hug and kiss on the head.

Oddly enough, as word of Chad's acrobatic skills from the bird feeder escapade spread throughout squirreldom, he received several invitations from *Squirrel du Soleil*, *Ringling Brothers*, and some random guy claiming to represent the estate and licensing for former daredevil *Evel Knievel*. Apparently the offers involved outlandish and particularly dangerous stunts, which Chad immediately dismissed out of hand…until the level of potential compensation caused him to at least hear them out. He was also intrigued by some of the flamboyant costumes.

Once details of Darryl's abilities were shared with the world, he received quite a bit of interest from several tech companies but ended up accepting a fellowship with a very prestigious think tank, the *American Squirrel*

Studies Institute. ASSI is a thought leader in advancing squirrel research and with Darryl's help has now embarked on a new educational initiative, which is focused on all aspects of squirrel safety including of course, preventing roadway incidents. One important initiative has been working with each of the major auto manufacturers to improve the sensitivity of their Advanced Driver Assistance Systems (ADAS). Specifically, Darryl developed a complex algorithm that uses artificial intelligence to interpret vehicle camera feeds and data from radar and lidar sensors for blind spot and front and rear collision avoidance. In a nutshell (sorry) Darryl's new advanced programming greatly improves the sensitivity and resulting accuracy of the detection systems so they can "see" objects with much greater precision. Yes, that includes even previously undetected small animals like squirrels, turtles, and snakes. I was pleased to hear his research caught the attention of engineers at *Tesla*, including the scientists and programmers that developed *Tesla's* autopilot feature. In fact, when Elon Musk heard about the increased accuracy and faster reaction time resulting from Darryl's programming enhancement, he created a new engineering task force specifically focused on front-facing, ground-hugging sensor technology to detect and instantly identify objects as low as two centimeters from the road surface and react only if the analysis reflects a lifeform is present. Musk's financial commitment, along with the financial support and full technical research resources of the institute, also has Darryl busy at work using artificial intelligence in training modules for young squirrels, something he calls *Project Artemis*. As an aside, he recently received a patent for a much more sophisticated version of his solar oven design and is a much sought-after speaker at technical innovation conferences.

As for me, there is still some controversy about what actually transpired following my auto accident, and I promised Christy I would refrain from further discussion on the topic, at least with her. I am a man of my word and have faithfully honored that pledge, but I do admit I occasionally drive very slowly past the community park… you know, just to appreciate the local wildlife.

Following my research regarding the squirrels, I was disappointed to find several of my journal article submissions documenting my findings were rejected by some of the most prestigious psychological publications, including *Qualitative Research in Psychology* and *Psychological Science in the Public Interest*. For whatever reason, it seems these well-respected journals chose not to accept the direct verbatim transcript of my verbal interactions with Sam and each member of the scurry. Why they elected to disregard the squirrels' direct comments, especially regarding their motivation for roadway incursions, is beyond me! An important component of psychological research is always direct observational assessment of the research subjects, which can provide valuable insight into the interactions with other members of the group, an opportunity to observe non-verbal cues and emotions, and in the case of the squirrels, how they react and relate to humans.

As crazy as it may sound, it is almost as though these esteemed research publications do not believe the comments in the transcript came from the squirrels themselves! Personally, I find that to be both disturbing and blatantly discriminatory. Maybe it's just me, but I really have to wonder if the same types of direct observational dialogue had come from, say dolphins, apes or other species regarded as "higher functioning", rather than creatures as common as squirrels, would they have been given more credibility and consideration? I suppose we will never know.

Fortunately, I can take solace in the fact that as I have traveled across the country on the current book tour and visited towns and neighborhoods from coast to coast, I often meet recent converts to the cause. Whether it is the woman who brought her pet squirrel to a book signing, a child wearing a *Give us a brake!* t-shirt, or a report of a nut vendor's skyrocketing sales at city parks, the word seems to be getting out. No, I can't honestly say I have seen a lot of *Squirrel Crossing* signs at potential problem intersections, but on my way to a *Nature Conservancy* rally in Ocala, Florida I did see a crew installing an additional flashing crosswalk signal activation button at a level just a few inches off the ground. It's the little things…

Finally, I am often asked what I learned from my research and the time I spent with the squirrels. I must confess I knew very little about these animals prior to this project and was initially motivated more out of anger than genuine concern for their wellbeing. I now have a unique appreciation for their quest for survival in the face of continued loss of habitat, predators, and other threats, including from humans and motor vehicles. Having gained so much from the experience, I can share several important takeaways, my "words of wisdom". Here is my "top ten" list:

1. The human mind is a wondrous thing, often crafting dreams in response to our needs, desires, and expectations.

2. When fantasy and reality overlap, that's when magic happens.

3. Even the most powerful and sophisticated technology, supercomputers, algorithms, and artificial intelligence are no substitute for direct personal observation, especially in nature.

4. If you can't depend on your cell phone to work when you need it most, you're basically screwed, and you'll just have to wing it.

5. If you are unfortunate enough to find yourself in the hospital, when you are discharged, be really careful with your meds. Otherwise, you might experience some pretty wacky shit.

6. There is nothing wrong with playing with your nuts, as long as you remember where you buried them, bless your heart.

7. If you ever find yourself talking to squirrels, it doesn't mean you are crazy. But it *might*.

8. My experience has been that when you are having a conversation with a squirrel and it mentions your nuts, it may have actually meant to convey that it thinks *you're nuts*. (Squirrels are not all that careful when it comes to grammar and sentence construction.)

9. Sometimes animals (like squirrels) venture into the roadway because they really *do* want to get to the other side.

10. When you see *any* animal in the road ahead, *please* do me a favor: *Give them a brake!* Yes, even *Suicide Squirrels*.

www.ingramcontent.com/pod-product-compliance
Lightning Source LLC
Chambersburg PA
CBHW071119170626
46809CB00002B/421